THE FREELAND VENDETTA

STONE CHALMERS
BOOK 1

RAYMUND EICH

TABLE OF CONTENTS

PROLOGUE

The operative crawled up the lifeless slope. Dust sneaked through the gaps between his helmet and his gillie suit, and sweat glued the dust to his neck and shoulders. Pebbles rolled between his chest and the ground. He sucked at a straw and hot water from a bag between his shoulders flooded his mouth.

At least the heat vents on the suit's front were open. Some of his body heat would slither between his chest and the baked ground. Enough to escape detection by the locals' decades-old IR sensors.

From over the top of the slope came the rumble of a large vehicle. He froze, arms and legs at odd angles. He sucked more hot water from the straw. The bag crinkled against his undershirt.

An overlay projected onto his field of vision by his transcranial stimulator reported no motion to his sides or behind him. If not for the vehicle, he could be the only person within fifty miles.

He crawled toward a rock the size and shape of a squashed basketball, straddling the contour line of the slope. Agonizingly slowly, giving the multicolored e-ink camouflage time to change patterns without a casual glance noticing. Finally he made it. He lay face down, inhaling warm air through slits in the sides of his helmet. The rock's narrow shadow covered the crown of his head. Barely cooler, but still a relief.

He subvoked a command to the computer implanted under the skin of his chest. A heat vent on the top of his helmet opened, dumping heat to the shade of the rock. Not much, but it would delay heat stroke a few seconds longer.

Another subvoked command. Diagnostics for his cameras, microphones, and volatile molecule sniffers whirled in his field of vision. All green. The implantable's static RAM could hold nearly an hour of data.

Time to look at the other side of the slope.

He closed the heat vent atop his helmet and slithered six inches sideways. Subvoked the commands to record on all channels. Lifted his head.

On the other side of the contour line, the ground sloped gently down to a field of pebbles and rocks in jumbled shades of khaki and pallid rust, scattered randomly by a billion years of wind and rain. Against the natural rockscape, a dull black structure of metal/carbon nanotube alloy, thirty yards long by ten wide and high, instantly revealed the hand of man.

The structure curved away from the operative, as if a robot with uneven wheels laid out the long sides during construction. The structure's long side facing him held double doors deeply recessed in the alloy wall. Near the far end, tiny holes in the alloy formed a grid about two yards square.

The operative's breath caught. His gaze completed the circle defined by the alloy walls. White spray paint drew a circle. *Estimated diameter 45 meters* appeared in his vision.

More sweat bloomed in his armpits and on his back. Estimate, hell. The circle's painters knew the intended diameter to the millimeter.

The men who'd built the structure and painted the circle also knew to hide their work from prying eyes. Thin poles staked around and throughout the circle held up a giant camouflage net, its sinuous surfaces rising from near ground level to simulate a low hillock. The nets glittered with strips of metal radar chaff.

Small wonder orbital surveillance had missed this site.

The operative breathed harder. His head wanted to jerk around, make sure the cameras caught everything. He resisted. Sudden movement might catch the attention of–

To the left. Half a mile from the curved structure, twenty men in woodland green camouflage scurried around a flatbed trailer bearing a red steel shipping container. The container was twin to a hundred million others carried by ship and truck and railroad around Earth and the colonies acceded to the Convention.

The halves of the container's top suddenly flipped open and struck the sides.

From the container's open top, a six-tube missile launcher emerged and swung its muzzles toward the curved structure. The clang of the opened top reached his hiding spot over the rocky ground. Fire streaked from the tubes. The missile launches shrieked in his ears.

Impact. Fireballs billowed into the cloudless sky. The explosion roared over the operative's hiding spot. The microphone's gain meter maxed out for a moment. Waves of hot wind stank of vaporized metal.

Sweat trickled down the operative's face. Plain as day what the locals trained for. Didn't they know the damage they would cause to their own planet?

They didn't care.

Smoke dissipated from the structure. Five gouges scarred the alloy wall facing the missile launcher. One missile had punched through the grid of tiny holes, leaving a jagged hole dripping with melted metal. Not enough to destroy the cooling system.

The men shouted among themselves. The operative couldn't hear their words, but from their tone, he imagined their expletives. Other than their shouts he only heard a faint buzz, like an insect near his ear.

Insect? No plants this far from the inhabited zone. Should mean no insects–

Something jabbed through his gillie suit into the back of his thigh. His heart slammed and he swatted his hand at whatever stuck him.

His arm turned into useless meat, dropping to the rocky ground. His head slumped, face-down onto the dust. Pebbles filled his vision like boulders, dim in the slivered light sneaking between the ground and his immobile head.

He tried wiggling his other arm. His legs. Nothing. He couldn't even turn his head. Paralyzed? Drugs could do that, delivered by dart–

How could he think so calmly? Yet he did. His heart pumped steadily, no faster than if he walked at an easy pace. His diaphragm rose and fell in a corresponding rhythm. He should panic... yet the thought skittered over the surface of his mind while his subconscious took its cues from his heart and respiration rates.

A paralyzing drug and sympathetic nervous system inhibitors. The locals knew their business.

The insect-like buzz became louder, then ended with a springy rattle about five feet to his right. An airborne drone landing, like a vulture.

Pebbles crunched on the rocky ground in the missile launcher's direction. Footsteps, several people. Coming his way. Far too close to have left the group at the missile launcher when the drone darted him. They'd tracked him, hid in camouflage twenty or thirty yards downs-lope. He'd looked right past them.

The footsteps resolved into three people. They fanned out around his head and halted.

"The Chinese man?" said a callow young man's voice in the twangy local accent, two yards to the left.

"Yup." Another man's voice, to the right. Hard-bitten as the dusty landscape.

Breaths heaved in and out of the young man. "I always heard tell Chinese were decent enough folks, if you got them out from under the reds."

From in front of the operative, a woman spoke, her voice melodious yet cold. "He serves a more evil master than the Chinese Communist Party."

The wind sighed, skittering dust.

"He serves the United Nations."

CHAPTER 1

Clouds brushed the tops of nearby highrises and flurried snow onto Marcus Garvey Park. Stone Chalmers stood at one end of the practice field with the six boys playing defensive back. They looked up at Stone through their wire mesh face shields and rubbed together their electrotouch gloves. Pale nine-year-old faces, cheeks red with cold, noses running.

"When's practice going to end?" Edwin muttered to Tiansheng. "I'm cold."

"Practice ends–" Stone said. Edwin lurched back, eyes full of whites. "–when head coach says it ends." Stone nodded toward the far end of the field. The team's head coach went along the offensive linemen, touching shoulders and padded blocking shields to make fine adjustments.

Nearer, twenty yards away, the other assistant coach thumped his free hand against a football. "Stone, ready?" he called.

Stone nodded. "Time for man coverage drills," he said to the boys. "Vikram, Hamza, you two first. Hang tight with the receivers and work on your breaks."

Vikram and Hamza nodded and trotted into position opposite two receivers. All four boys looked like blue marshmallow men in heavily padded uniforms and concussion-resistant helmets. Green diagnostic LEDs on chests and backs showed all the players' tag force sensors in working order.

"Hut, hut!" the other assistant coach called. The receivers took off. Hamza's man sprinted straight downfield on a fly route. Hamza pivoted and ran shoulder-to-shoulder with him.

The other receiver ran five yards, then cut in. Vikram backpedaled until the cut in, then closed–and the receiver cut again and raced toward the end zone.

Vikram twisted, lost momentum. Five yards of separation. The other assistant coach tossed a tight spiral arcing into the receiver's hands.

Stone stuck out his arm and caught the receiver across the chest. He patted the boy's helmet with his other hand. The soft plastic firmed up under his palm. "Good cuts. Hand me the ball." Stone tossed the ball to the other assistant coach. "Bryce, Gonzalo, your turn."

The two boys ran toward the line of scrimmage. Gonzalo held out his hand to low-five Vikram. Vikram trudged along, shoulders hunched and head down, and missed the gesture.

Vikram came closer and looked up at Stone. His eyes crinkled, ready to cry. "I tried to work on my break, Coach Stone."

Stone pulled him into a hug and rubbed his helmet. "It's fine. Practice makes progress. Keep at it, you'll get it."

Vikram nodded. He walked, head raised, to his place in line. Stone watched him go and the cold sensation of lying washed down Stone's throat. In his mind's eye appeared his great-grandfather, Trajanus Chalmers, his Mexico City Conquistadors cap precariously balanced on his graying waves. A slow head shake, a glint in his yellow eyes, and Paw-Paw said *You can't coach hips*.

Stone drew in a lungful of chill air. None of these boys would grow up to become football players–lack of hips was the least of their shortcomings. Boys from the glass-faced carbon-nanotube highrises north of Central Park, sons of UN and non-governmental organization officials, they faced more important futures than playing football. The burden of maintaining the galaxy's fragile order would soon fall on them.

The team's shortest, slowest receiver ran two steps, then turned back and caught a pass. Gonzalo shoved him, both hands in the receiver's back. The LED on the receiver's back turned red.

Stone clapped. "Way to close on him," he called to Gonzalo.

A ding sounded in Stone's ear. Against Mount Morris' exposed gray schist and the brown trunks of leafless maples, bright green letters appeared. Not memory—neural activity induced by a network of nanometer-wide wires grown around his hair follicles and linked to the worldweb.

Come to office immediately. 108 on Freeland. Out.

Stone blew out a streamer of breath. The sender lacked any need to identify himself. Only Gray could force a message past Stone's software assistant.

The burden of maintaining the galaxy's fragile order now fell on him.

He raised his hand and the six defensive backs looked up at him. "Boys, I hate to do this, but I'm being called into work."

A chorus of groans. Edwin's eyes drooped. "Can't they send someone else?"

Stone cocked his head and smiled, mouth closed. "When you're good at your job, you're in demand." He patted Edwin and Tiansheng on their shoulder pads. "Later."

He subvoked to his car, *Pull up on Madison just before 123rd.* He jogged over and told the other assistant coach he had to leave. Twenty yards further, the head coach looked up from the padded thud of offensive linemen blocking pass rushers. "Let me guess," he said to Stone. "Work needs you?"

"Afraid so."

"You'll make the game on Saturday?"

108 meant an agent dead on an operation.

"Tricky negotiation on the far side of a wormhole. Plan on me being gone."

He strode away from the field and between the gray stone pillars flanking the park's gate on the Madison side near 123rd. Cars whispered uptown, headlights on under the overcast sky.

Claws scratched the sidewalk and collar tags jingled. Brown eyes bulged in a stout Boston terrier's black and white face. No leash.

Every three steps, the dog angled its head up and left, mark of a gene-tech'd and conditioned urge to seek commands from its mistress.

The dog's owner had a pale heart-shaped face between the upturned collar of her black leather kneecoat and the cultured gray fur trim of her red bucket hat. Stone flicked his gaze up and down her lean form, then looked past her down Madison. He shook his left forearm and his watch slid past the cuff of his blue tracksuit. Platinum bezel and hands, silicon wafer face, a half-carat diamond marking twelve o'clock. Only a woman would notice how expensive it was from five yards away.

Three-forty-five. Her soles clacked closer and a floral perfume trickled into his nose. He took a closer look at her. A snowflake fell in front of her crisp cheekbones and narrow nose. She tucked blond tips of hair under her hat and her gaze met his.

Pretty, but a thousand women as pretty arrived in the city every day, dreaming their social justice degrees from flyover-state public universities and second-tier Ivies prepared them to change the world.

Stone smiled weakly and looked through her, down Madison. She sniffed in a breath. The dog trotted between its mistress and Stone and made a low growl.

Moments later, a sleek black coupe with tinted windows, its faces as sharp as a supermodel's cheekbones, parked itself at the curb. A faint snick and the coupe's doors popped open. He grabbed the handle and pulled too firmly for the pneumatic assist to help him.

Inside, Stone eased back on the horseshoe-shaped leather seat. "UNICA," he said. "Priority one."

The coupe accelerated smoothly and cut across three lanes to turn east on 123rd. Small, blocky cars in front of him slid left and right to the curb. Another right turn and the coupe headed downtown on Lexington. Stone's car weaved in and out of traffic and all the lights turned green.

Spanish Harlem gave way to the Upper East Side. The highrises here stood taller, with stone faces and architectural curlicues at street level. In the upper 60s Stone caught a glimpse of the Korean hot dog stand in front of his apartment building. His coupe accelerated, pushing him back against the cushions. His mouth watered thinking of a hot dog with kimchi.

No telling what the locals ate on Freeland.

The snow flurried more heavily here. He would wake to a dirty slush if he remained in the city till morning. South of 59th, logos of UN agencies and NGOs marked a building or two on every block. Pedestrians wore the native costumes of two hundred countries, tailored and adapted to New York chic, and strode through the concrete canyons as if they worked at the most important jobs in the galaxy.

Stone's lower face flexed in a smile that failed to reach his eyes. Let them imagine they mattered. Delusions of importance kept them out of his hair.

At first glance, UNICA headquarters looked like any other of the thousand skyscrapers occupied by the agencies and organizations that governed mankind. UNICA's eighty-story highrise filled the middle of a block in the mid 50s between Lexington and the FDR. Concrete bollards, and Czech hedgehogs like a giant's steel jacks, lined the sidewalk. A sign perpendicular to the sidewalk between the parking garage entrance and exit bore a dusting of snow. On the sign, four multiracial hands clasped one another, superimposed over the UN flag. Fine print below the image read *United Nations Interagency Coordination Authority.*

The gate bobbed up. Stone's coupe entered the garage.

Eight minutes later, he strode from the elevator on the 27th floor and entered the office of the most powerful man alive.

Essentially all six billion survivors of the Time of Troubles assumed the Secretary-General governed the world. He or she appeared on Worldforum, after all, when time came to call on the US to send soldiers to enforce a resolution, and the US President always complied. Even the vast majority of UN and NGO workers trodding the nearby streets assumed the same.

A few thousand people, more perceptive of the invisible ebbs and flows of power behind the public show, might understand the head of UNICA wielded far more power. The bland bureaucratic label–UN Interagency Coordination Authority–hid the fact that every major decision by the UN's agencies and the major NGOs required the assent of

UNICA Director Kroebel, high in his opulent corner office facing Central Park from the skyscraper's penthouse.

Stone and a dozen other people knew Director Kroebel took his orders from UNICA's assistant director of operational planning. Gray.

The ceiling-height door stood six inches open, showing a swathe of bookcases and windows. Stone rapped his knuckles on the manufactured wood.

Gray's voice boomed through the opening. "Come in."

Stone entered and shut the door behind him.

In profile at a standing workstation, Gray peered through reading glasses down his long nose at text scrolling up one of three monitors. Too mature a man for new-fangled transcranial nerve induction technologies, or at least that's what he wanted his few subordinates to think.

Gaze locked on his monitors, Gray raised his right hand, a patrol leader commanding his men to halt. "I need a moment." He angled his head at another monitor. Checking the time. "Pour us each a drink."

A table of cherry wood and gold inlay. Whisky lurked in a decanter, next to a stack of clean glasses. Stone lifted the decanter's hefty glass stopper, poured. The peaty smell evoked his father, numbing himself as he dissolved over the years into his worn, brown leather recliner. He stoppered the decanter and cracked open a bottle of sparkling water for himself. Stone held his hissing, mineral-scented water near his nose, then slipped between visitor seats and set the whisky on Gray's second, sitting-height desk, near an embedded touchscreen facing an empty ergonomic chair.

The text window winked out. "Enough of that," Gray said. He pivoted a quarter turn, revealing his broad shoulders, firm chest, and narrow waist. His blue tie, properly dimpled, arched away from his starched white shirt. Under his high forehead, his gray eyes, source of his code name, took in Stone's blue tracksuit. "Any future Giants players on your team?"

"Don't bet on it."

"You know I never bet. Sit, and tell me about Freeland." Gray extended his index finger straight up. "No searches."

"I didn't search the web about that colony when I drove downtown. Why would I now?"

Gray's eyes narrowed. "You are a very good operative, Stone. If you kept up with analyst reports, you could be a great one."

He said that every time. Stone eased into a seat. "Freeland is the forty-second and most recent extrasolar colony to accede to the Dubai Convention. Two, three months back, ITB–" The UN's Interstellar Transport Bureau. "–sited the Earth end of the wormhole somewhere in Texas. I've run out of facts."

"Speculations, then?"

Stone squinted past Gray at a painting of two racing sailboats on the wall. Blurred lines and peach-colored dollops of faces filled the painting with excitement. Fifteen years of visits to Gray's office, and Stone still didn't know if Gray sailed every weekend, or hated the ocean and wanted to misdirect his few visitors.

His gaze met Gray's eyes. "From calling themselves 'Freelanders', I'll guess they were Libertarians or Objectivists who fled the U.S.A. during the Time of Troubles on a warpdrive ship."

"Accurate, except for the colony's ideological bent. Its founders were Czech Texans. They established the colony on explicitly ethnic grounds."

"Yes, and?" Stone drank. Sparkling water fizzed across his tongue. "Most colonies are monoethnic–"

"The Freeland charter limits immigration to people who genetically are at least 25% Czech and at least 75% white. Here's the full text." Gray touched the tips of his index and middle fingers to the screen embedded in his desk, then flicked them forward.

A bong sounded in Stone's ears. A text notification of the received file popped into his vision, then faded.

"Seventy-five percent white." Those thousand women coming to the city with social justice degrees would shake with outrage. Utter a few well-practiced words and in fifteen minutes they would climb into his bed to punish those distant racists. "Yet Freeland acceded to the Dubai Convention anyway."

Gray lifted his whisky glass. "ITB's quite skilled at persuading colony worlds that granting 10% of their habitable land surfaces to the

UN for new settlement is in their best interests. The standard ploys worked on Freeland. ITB sold the colony's business leaders on new employees and customers. It promised the governor and other elected politicians consulting jobs after they leave office. One legislator had enough principle to raise the charter's immigration terms. ITB told him the land grant, by law, would belong to the UN, so Freeland's charter would not apply. They assuaged him further by inviting him to UN headquarters to provide Freelander input on any settlement plans."

Stone drank more sparkling water. A hundred governments in the underdeveloped world sought dumping grounds for their undesirables–quarrelsome religious and ethnic minorities, unemployed college graduates, excess males arising from sex-selection technologies. Anything to forestall a repeat of the Time of Troubles. ITB's wormhole network made vast landscapes, dozens of light years away in real space, reachable in a few days of travel across Earth. ITB might bring Freeland's representative to meet a few ambassadors in the Secretariat building, but it would do the colonist no good. Bureaucrats in a dozen UN agencies would decide the fate of his world.

"The Freelanders will be in for a shock," Stone said, "when they find out what they signed up for."

Gray sipped, then set down his whisky with a resonant thump. "They already know."

CHAPTER 2

Stone arched an eyebrow. "A desk jockey downstairs spun up a good story, at least."

Gray narrowed his eyes. "I know the personnel in Analysis Branch. Far better than you. Here are vetted facts they gave me." He jutted out a finger with each one. "One: within a week of the colony's accession to the Dubai Convention, hundreds of colonists on social media accused their leaders of bringing to Freeland all the evils their ancestors fled last century. Or to quote, 'ghettos and barrios.' Two: colonists spray painted the house of the CEO of Freeland's largest construction company with the slogan *Just say No to criminals and welfare queens.* Three: a week ago, an unidentified perpetrator threw a rock through the classroom window of the governor's youngest son. The rock bore a laser-carved message: *We will kill your son to protect our daughters from Earth's thugs.*"

"People settled in their ways assume the worst of any change." Stone took a mineral swallow of sparkling water. A chill washed down him.

Even if the Freelanders assumed their way of life would be violated, colonists on other worlds had done the same without threatening businessmen and politicians. "Though never before to this extent," Stone added.

"Quite." Gray's tone sounded like centuries of wind down Manhattan's concrete canyons. "Reason enough to draw my attention. Yet the situation could be even worse than a spontaneous outbreak of populism. One of the Freeland leaders who signed the Dubai Convention may have leaked details to trigger the outbreak." Gray lifted his whisky glass and swirled it in long, knobby fingers. His hand grew still, but he did not speak until the brown liquid calmed. "Or UN advance personnel on the planet betrayed Earth's plans."

"That's impossible."

"Improbable, I'll grant you. In my position, though, I must consider every possibility. Even the worst."

Stone nodded. "Which is why you sent–?"

"Dragon."

"Dragon? You sent an East Asian operative to a planet where his ethnicity isn't welcome?"

Gray sipped. "A calculated risk. On Earth, certainly, northern European whites view Asians more favorably than other ethnicities. I considered it likely Freelanders would as well. He went under the cover story of a luxury adventure travel blogger scouting undiscovered tourist sites for rich Earthers. He received some odd looks but, overall, hospitable treatment. The prospect of making money helps people overcome their ethnic biases."

"Not everyone, apparently."

"After three weeks in the capital, Dragon headed into the wilds. Under the pretext of exploring a wilderness adventure site, he followed a lead regarding weapons training by disgruntled locals. Evidence pointed to the locals being bankrolled by a Freelander transport mogul named Lukas Benavides."

"'Benavides' doesn't sound Czech."

Gray shrugged. "Perhaps he lied about his ancestry to get on board the settler ships. Immaterial. Benavides is the bioseeding patron of eight hundred thousand acres of wilderness, which includes the site Dragon investigated."

"Where Benavides and his men killed him?"

Gray shook his head. "Our field office on Freeland tracked Dragon's biotelemetry and his SUV's positioning beacon back to the city. An hour later, he died in his hotel room. An hour after that, the local medical examiner logged death by natural causes. Another hour, and Dragon's remains were cremated."

"Did biotelemetry show any signs of struggle? Heart rate spike, accelerometer signals...."

Gray's unsmiling face answered *no*.

Stone swallowed dryly. "His abductors knew we remotely monitored his biometrics." UN personnel betraying Earth's plans–and Gray's agents–suddenly became less improbable.

He took a long drink of sparkling water, composing himself while the fizz and mineral taste flooded his mouth. He lowered the glass. His cheeks tightened in a smirk of easy confidence. "My mission is all three, right?"

"All three?"

"Determine Dragon's cause of death, follow his weapons training lead, and find the source of the Freelanders' opposition to Earth. Right?"

Gray nodded. "We've prepared your cover. Hypnogogue it on the flight to Texas. You leave from LaGuardia in two hours."

Stone downed the last of his sparkling water, then shifted his weight forward in his chair. "If that's all, I'll go upstairs for my cover–"

"Not all. Before you download your cover files and pick up the supporting trinkets, go to Genomics Sub-branch. 30th floor."

Stone blinked. Never been there before.

"One final thing. When you arrive at Freeland, avoid our field office, both in person and electronically. Surveillance of the office by hostiles possibly tipped them to Dragon's true role."

Or someone in the field office betrayed Earth's plans–and Stone's fellow agent. A glance at Gray's suddenly creased face kept the words out of Stone's mouth. The old man realized the possibility. He didn't need a reminder.

"Got it." Stone's legs pushed him out of his chair. "One more question. How many of ITB's Keyhole Kops are on Freeland?"

"Too many," Gray said. "I assumed I needn't tell you to avoid them as well."

ITB's undercover operatives supposedly only worked in wormhole security and operations. Supposedly. Like cockroaches, bureaucratic mission creep had survived the Time of Troubles. "Don't worry. I'll keep my distance. They would only get in my way."

"I've never seen a SNP profile like yours," the Genomics tech said. A rubber band in the back bundled her blond hair. Her full face was almost as pale as her white lab coat. A faint pink glowed in her cheeks, was not painted on. In his younger days, Stone would have glanced once and crossed her off his target list.

Not that she was on his target list now. She and her spinning, rolling stool seemed fused together, as if she never left this cramped laboratory. Computer cooling fans hummed and liquids sloshed inside the base of an upright, man-sized plastic tank occupying the far corner.

Off his target list, but he had skills to practice in case he needed them on Freeland. "I bet you say that to all the men." Stone curled up the corners of his mouth and held his gaze on her brown eyes for a two-count. He looked away. In the westward windows, his reflection grinned back against the backdrop of darkening sky and high-rises with glowing windows, like pixelated jack-o-lanterns.

"No," the Genomics tech said. Her voice lacked guile. "Yours is unique. Is your ancestry why you took the codename Hybrid?"

Stone replied slowly, in a lecturing voice, "I prefer the term 'person of multiraciality.'" That line would wrongfoot his usual women, get them gushing apologies for offending him, conceding the lead to him in the mating dance. He smirked and wished he could laugh.

"I've never heard that term. Anyway, your codename definitely fits your SNP profile."

"I'd comment, if I knew what a–snip?–profile was." He curled up the corners of his mouth again.

"Oh." She blinked at him as if she saw him for the first time. "You know what genes are, at least?"

He nodded. "Blueprints for proteins."

The Genomics tech eased out a breath. "Good. Okay. The genetic code contains a lot of redundancies. Because of that, there are I don't know how many trillion different gene sequences that can provide the blueprint for one protein. Since those different gene sequences lead to the same result, there's essentially no selective pressure to weed them out of the gene pool. But they also don't mutate very often. So you have a bunch of single nucleotide polymorphisms, SNPs, you inherited, and your SNP profile tells us with high accuracy about your ancestors. Got it?"

No, but saying the word aloud would only get a longer and more detailed explanation. "How is my profile unique?"

A negotiation between his software assistant and hers poked at the bottom of his mind. The poke went away and a pie chart popped into his vision to the left of her pale face. "You're 9.4% African."

The boys would still be at the park, doing coverage drills and working on their breaks. "A great-grandfather of mine played cornerback in the NFL for fourteen years."

"I've never heard of the game of cornerback, and I don't know where the NFL is," the Genomics tech said. "You're also 6.3% Ashkenazi."

"One of my great-grandmothers was a prominent Reform rabbi."

"And 12.5% Spanish."

"Another of my great-grandfathers. Born in Mexico, was an anchorman for a Spanish-language television network's national news broadcast in the U.S. I get my blond hair from him." Again, a line to wrongfoot his usual women.

The Genomics tech swept her finger around three-fourths of the pie chart. "The rest of your ancestry is northwest European. You already meet most of the requirement."

"Requirement?"

"You're already 75% white. Before you leave the lab, I'm supposed to make you 25% Czech."

"My grandparents made that impossible, decades ago."

"Not Czech in any real sense," she said. "Just SNPs in the parts of your body conveniently used for DNA samples. Time for you to get naked."

Stone raised his eyebrow. "You haven't even taken me out for coffee, let alone dinner."

"The CRISPR dermal vector requires exposure to all your skin." She blinked at him. "Oh, you're embarrassed. I'll leave the room, then you can get naked and step into the vessel." She spun her stool and turned her head toward the man-sized plastic tank in the corner. "The vessel will beam text and verbal instructions through your transcranial stimulator web. Follow them. The process will go faster. Got it?"

The cover story waiting for him required him to pass as a potential immigrant to Freeland. He gave one sharp nod. "No time like the present." He pinched his tracksuit's zipper pull and tugged it down his chest.

The Genomics tech fixed her guileless brown eyes on him. "Good, you're not letting any little fears get in the way. The vessel will let me know if you need my help. Bye, Hybrid." She separated from the rolling stool and went to the door. Denim swished between her thighs with each step.

Stone loped off his stool and across the laboratory. The tank stood in the corner like a rocket on the launchpad. He ran his hand over its stippled, beige plastic surface. Air puffed and a fine seam popped an inch open.

He shed his clothes and piled them on a lab bench, next to a stack of folded white towels. He rested his watch on his tracksuit. A draft chilled his bare skin.

Stone stepped up into the tank and pulled an inside handle. The door swung shut, trapping him in a space six inches wider than his shoulders. LEDs spaced evenly around the ceiling and floor dimly lit a smooth white plastic interior punched through by two dozen nozzles. A synthetic female voice said *Rotate the handle ninety degrees clockwise to lock.*

He turned the handle a quarter-turn. A click from the door echoed inside the vessel.

A motor whirred near his left shoulder, opening a compartment between two nozzles. Inside, a milky blue liquid filled an inch-high disposable plastic cup. *Swish the liquid in your mouth for thirty seconds, then swallow.*

Stone swished berry and mint and bitter medicinal flavors around his mouth. He turned his head and a timer in the lower right corner of his vision moved with him. *4. 3. 2. 1.* His nose wrinkled as the clashing tastes went down his throat.

The compartment motor whirred again. Same milky blue liquid, but this time in a battery-powered syringe with a green button at the back and a flexible, glistening tube on the business end. *Insert anally until tube is fully extended, then deploy the liquid.*

"You haven't taken me out for dinner, either."

Two seconds of silence, then *Insert anally until tube is fully extended, then deploy–*

Stone grabbed the syringe. The tube glistened with lubricant. He grimaced and eased the tube into his backside. It extended itself inside his rectum like a parasitic worm. He moved the syringe body closer to his body, until cold plastic bumped against his skin.

A green checkmark appeared in his vision. *Depl–*

By feel, he pressed the button. Liquid squirted into his colon.

Stone yanked out the syringe and threw it to the floor. He squirmed his hips until the crawling liquid in his colon faded below perception.

He took a breath, blew it out. Better than getting shot.

Once again the motor sounded. The compartment door revealed a syringe, identical to the first.

"How thoughtful of you," Stone said to the tank. "You saved the best for last."

Insert the catheter–

"Got it." He picked up the syringe, gritted his teeth. When he pressed the button, the liquid burned like a venereal disease or a urinary tract infection. He squeezed his eyes shut and grunted.

After a time, the pain faded. He lifted his shoulders and breathed more easily.

Dermal vector delivery begins in 3. 2. 1.

Cold jets of the blue liquid needled him all over. The synthetic female voice told him to turn his body a few degrees and hold each position for five seconds. He almost got used to the jets striking patches of skin when time came to expose fresh nerve endings. Shivers gripped him. He pulled his arms closer to his flanks–

Hold arms away from body.

Stone did. Cold seeped into his armpits. Between his legs. Through his hair. Down his back. Hold. Turn. Hold.

The jets cut off. *You may exit now.*

Stone spun the handle counter-clockwise with trembling hands and pushed. He staggered to the bench. Clumsily he pulled towels of the stack, dropping one on the floor. Plush fabric, still faintly warm from a clothes dryer.

A few minutes later, dry and not shivering, he put his tracksuit back on and snapped his watch to his wrist. Twinges still ran through his lower abdomen. No help for it.

He headed out of the room. In the corridor, the Genomics tech stared at the wall and molded the air with both hands. Some data manipulation through her transcranial stimulator only she could see.

She glanced over her shoulder, then swiped her right hand palm-down in front of her and turned. "Looks like you followed instructions."

"Best to get it over with."

She nodded. "After your mission, come back and we'll restore the SNP profile in the target tissues back to your original."

"Thanks, but I might stick with being a quarter Czech."

The Genomics tech made a quarter-turn away, but then her eyebrows jutted up and she raised her right hand. "Oh. Almost forgot. The vector delivered by catheter only changes the SNP profile of the cells lining your bladder and urethra. Your sperm cells retain your original SNP profile. Too complicated to change them. Very invasive even if we could. So use a condom when you're in the field."

The last traces of any urge to bed the Genomics tech evaporated, but a mild affection remained. "Gee, thanks, sis."

"And flush it right away. If you blow your cover because you leave contradictory DNA evidence tied up in a plastic bag, don't blame me."

"Don't worry, I won't." He shook his wristwatch past his cuff, glanced down. "I'd love to chat more, but I have a plane to catch."

CHAPTER 3

Five minutes later, Stone knocked on an ajar door on the 29th floor. An LED display on the wall next to the door frame read *Operational Support I*. Cover stories.

Before anyone inside replied, he pushed the door wide and strode in.

One end of an L-shaped room. A wall-to-wall counter of sand-colored cultured stone separated the waiting area in which he stood from a maze of gray cubicles disguising the room's full depths.

A head and upper torso peeked out from behind a cubicle panel. A man, woolly eyebrows and a peaked nose. Unfamiliar. "Hybrid?"

Stone nodded.

"I'll be with you in a sec." The man receded, then emerged from the cubicle farm with a transparent plastic folio dangling between long fingers. Tall yet slouched, he approached, then flicked the folio onto the counter. A perfect toss. The folio landed flat and rotated a quarter-turn to stop with its zippered end near Stone.

"We haven't met," Stone said.

"Fabrizio."

"Are you new?" The assured way Fabrizio had tossed the folio onto the counter suggested the answer was no.

"I've been here six years. You?"

How long Stone had served was no business of a cover stories tech. "Jürgen usually does prep for me. Is he off today?"

Fabrizio puckered his lips, shook his head. "No. He's been promoted. I moved up into his former position." He drummed his hands on the cultured stone. "Good hunting." He turned for the cubicle maze and soon disappeared.

Stone rolled his eyes, then reached for the transparent folio. Inside, a manila envelope lay on the counter, its color roughly matching the surface, like a moth's protective coloration. Stone unzipped the folio and shook out the envelope. Along with the envelope, a white plastic object half the size of his little finger tinkled onto the counter.

He squeezed the sides of the plastic object. A clip on the back snicked its jaws apart. Stone zipped open his tracksuit and clipped the plastic object to his undershirt near his implantable computer.

Within a minute he descended in the express elevator. Pressure filled his ears, muffling a mellow instrumental version of some shrieking violent song from the Time of Troubles. As if the world had truly mellowed in the last decades. He pinched the manila envelope between thumb and forefinger and spun it a quarter-turn up and down. Inside the envelope, a rigid plastic cylinder clattered against metal objects.

His coupe waited in the parking garage outside the elevator lobby. He climbed in and it pulled out of the garage and into traffic. Stop-and-go rush hour traffic all the way up Third, and time enough to make his flight without overriding city traffic control. He rested his hand on the manila envelope, lying next to him on the rear seat. The thick paper passed the outlines of data chips and keys to his hand. Curious, but the artifacts relating to his cover would make more sense to him if he opened the envelope later.

When Stone entered his apartment, he locked the door behind him and let his eyes adjust. The glow of a thousand high-rises through the windows, partially reflected by off-white wallboard, cast thin light on the dark fabrics and straight lines of his living room furniture. The tomb of a Scandinavian pharaoh, a brunette with high cheekbones declared his apartment to be one morning, a few minutes before he never saw her again. To the right, behind Stone's dark, dusty kitchen, old Mr. Leipziger in the next apartment banged a pot on the induction cooktop.

Stone subvoked to his implantable, *I need clothes for the climate around Freeland's wormhole mouth..*

He crossed the dark living room. His bedroom windows showed matte black, and a single bulb glowed in his closet. The scent of cedar oil bit his nose as he approached. Panels as deep as the closet divided it into eight floor-to-ceiling storage cubbies. Each cubby held a roller carryon case, a pair of shoes and a change of clothes hanging from a bar. The single bulb glowed over the third cubby from the left.

Khaki tactical pants, a rust-red polo shirt with a golfer icon over the breast, and a thin, baggy black jacket. He shucked off his tracksuit, pulled the polo over his undershirt. Warmer, dryer weather than the city, and the disguise should suffice. The garments only put him at risk of a golfer bending his ear.

As for other risks.... Stone strapped on his shoulder and ankle holsters, then knelt beside his bed. He reached under and his fingers slid onto the keys of his firearm safe and flexed, entering the combination. The drawer hissed open, then the motor hummed, sliding the drawer into view. Stone slid his .357 pistol into the shoulder holster and two magazines of cartridges into zippered pockets on his tactical pants. His hand nearly engulfed the compact 9mm and he snapped it into the ankle holster.

In the living room, he pulled on the black jacket and reached in the same motion for the doorknob.

His coupe flashed its hazards in the pickup zone outside his building. Shivering, Stone hopped in while the doorman loaded his roller case. The coupe crawled up First and onto FDR Drive, where the computerized reflexes of self-driving cars, freed of pedestrian traffic, picked up speed. Snowflakes landed one-by-one on the windshield. The heater, finally up to temperature, soon turned them into trickles of water. He took the Triborough over the dark sports fields and the fusion power plant on Randalls Island, across the dull chop of the East River. The Brooklyn neighborhoods on either side of the parkway, the destinations of the other cars in Queens and Long

Island, all were foreign to him. He might as well be driving across Kansas.

Minutes later, Stone's black coupe pulled up at LaGuardia. The long, curved, overhang of the terminal building blocked the snow flurry. A robotic cart rolled up and the coupe popped its trunk. A plane's engines roared on the other side of the terminal.

Inside, Stone slipped through crowds of average Americans, rumpled businessmen off to Chicago or Denver, shell-shocked tourists returning to flyover country. The terminal smelled of hot dry air and the oiled submachineguns of the TSA security police. He cut across the line shuffling toward the X-ray machines and brain scanners at the main security checkpoint. Only five others waited ahead of him at the prescreened, elite passenger security line.

When his turn came, he laid his roller case on the conveyor belt. Thumb against the scanner, he waited for the green light and cheerful bing, then strode ahead. The metal detector looked like a dumb box of plastic, but it had enough networked computer power for Gray's hackers to suborn it. Stone went through, pistol and magazines unre-marked by the blue-jacketed TSA. The roller case's wheels whispered over worn tile.

He boarded soon after reaching the gate. First class, a window seat, next to a businessman in a sweater vest gesturing and subvoking in an intense conversation. Stone pulled the manila envelope from his roller case, along with a black velvet eyemask and a pinkie-sized tube of earplugs, and tossed them onto his seat before hefting the case into the overhead.

Seated, he opened the manila envelope. Without looking, he fished inside for the rigid plastic cylinder. A pharmacy bottle, complete with a false patient name, false prescription, false pharmacy address. The cocktail of tablets rattled inside. He raised his hand for the flight atten-dant's attention, made a W with his fingers, tapped the side of his hand to his chin.

A moment later, she set a water bottle on his tray table. Stone emptied the pharmacy bottle into his free hand. Two tablets and a capsule, color-coded green, yellow, red. He popped the green one in his mouth and chased it down with a swig of water.

A puff of white vapor crossed Stone's vision. The businessman lowered a nicotine vaporizer from his mouth and peered at Stone's hand. "What's all that?"

"Without these, I'm a white knuckle flier," Stone lied.

The businessman took another puff of nicotine vapor, then lifted a glass clinking with ice, smelling of gin. "Enough of these will do the same, and they're free."

Only fools used any drug that made them less effective, instead of more. Stone waggled his head side-to-side. "They won't do the same. Not for me. I'll be asleep most of the flight. I usually don't snore."

"My wearable runs a noise-canceling app. Linked with my transcranial stim mesh." The businessman squinted at the sleepmask and tube of earplugs. "More effective at blocking out sound than using that stuff."

"Again, not for me." Stone popped the yellow capsule. In went the earplugs, muffling sound. Pulled the sleepmask's elastic cord around his head, left the mask itself over his forehead.

The red tablet. He pulled the sleepmask over his eyes. His hand, suddenly heavy, tapped the white plastic object clipped to his undershirt. The rattling ice in the businessman's glass sounded grew even more distant. Stone's hand slid down his torso and settled in his lap.

Stone lost consciousness before the plane pulled away from the gate.

He woke up with two personalities crammed into his skull.

Adrenaline kicked him in the back. Chest heaving, he yanked at the sleepmask. His fingertips pushed taut the skin of his forehead. He pawed at the sleepmask and finally slid it up.

A spacious airline seat. A reclining businessman in a sweater vest snored next to him, tray table laden with a glass of melting ice and empty vape cartridges.

The hell? He'd climbed into his pickup truck at the Society's headquarters in Austin for the drive to the wormhole mouth–

His mind shifted. Two selves came clear within him, like that time at NYU he and three classmates popped neuroactive drugs before their method acting class. The real one solidified, like a ghost resolving into flesh. Rolston Wentworth Gridley "Stone" Chalmers, UNICA operative. Spy, killer, seducer of more women than he could count. The other personality was merely data from the clip-on transfer unit, hypnogogued into his mind by the drug cocktail and his implantable computer.

Stone probed the other personality with his thoughts.

Jasper Jezhek, a family name to match the snips crispered into his genes. Employee of the Pan-American Czech and Slovak Cultural Preservation Society, headquartered in Austin, Texas. A name, a job. Insufficient on their own... and memories came like waves rolling up a beach.

Herding bull calves to dad and older brothers for castration, linking arms and swaying with thirty thousand other students after a Texas A&M football victory, staring wistfully out an office building's window at a summer sky full of clouds like puffed cotton, drinking bock beer and peering at nametags in a Society gathering in a dusty barbecue joint full of slanting afternoon light and monaural recordings of western swing. Lament tinged them all. Another memory, the flag-draped coffin of one older brother, dead in some failed nation-building mission somewhere on Earth.

Lament ebbed. Purpose straightened Stone's back. Persuade Freeland's leaders to invite thousands of Society members to their planet. For both sides' benefit, against the foreign millions the UN would inflict on Freeland.

Stone cycled deep breaths in and out. Jasper Jezhek faded from his awareness, but remained as certain as his skill at shooting a pistol or driving a car. He pulled out his earplugs, then slid the manila envelope from the seatback pocket. He reached in and outlines of objects against his fingertips filled him with recognition, more. Familiarity. A college class ring, retrieved from the bottom of a tall glass of beer in a centuries-old custom. A keychain empty but for a bottle opener with the Texas A&M logo. A flat metal case about two inches by three, cool to the touch. Business cards. He visualized the Society's logo and the animated slideshow of Texas landscapes on the cards despite having never seen them. Business cards, utterly archaic.

As archaic as Freeland's quest for ethnic purity.

He dropped the business card case back into the manila envelope. Pressure jabbed his ears. Stone held his nose and closed his mouth, exhaled. The whine of the plane's engines came louder. So too did the businessman's snores.

More pressure in his ears. Stone looked out the window. Dark subdivisions below, street lamps partially screened by old trees. The highrises of downtown Houston glittered twenty miles to his left. Insanely hot and humid in summer, late autumn would make it more comfortable.

Thirty minutes later, Stone's words tasted as thick and warm as the air outside the terminal. He pulled his roller case to the taxi stand. Sweat dampened the small of his back before a taxi popped its door and trunk for him.

Cracked leather squeaked under his backside and conditioned air smothered him. His implantable popped a business' name and address into his field of vision. "R & G Customs," he told the taxi, along with an address a mile from the airport.

The taxi delivered him to a complex of light industrial buildings, all one story high with pitted concrete walls. Next to the parking lot entrance, a bronze sculpture of a smith—one of a million cast in one of a thousand foundries around the world, according to a randomized pattern ensuring each was unique—hammered a sword into a plowshare atop a pedestal showing business names. Another sculpture, a bronze-casted surveyor looking through a tripod-mounted monocular, stood on thick grass near the front door of R & G Customs.

A wall-mounted video panel and the smell of stale coffee dominated a tiny waiting area. The video panel flicked away from a football highlight show, Mexico City versus Toronto, to a computer-generated receptionist, blond and blue-eyed as a girl from Jasper Jezhek's home town. "May I have your name?"

"Gray sent me." Stone widened his left eye toward the screen. Light flashed.

The computer-generated image froze, then skipped ahead a dozen frames. "Our sales representative will be with you shortly."

Football highlights returned. Mexico City's cornerback bit on a play fake. The ball spiraled over his head and the Toronto receiver caught it in full stride. Stone sniffed out a breath as the receiver high-stepped into the end zone. *You can't coach hips, but you can coach watching your man instead of the quarterback's eyes.*

An interior door opened. A pudgy man came out, mouth tight under a ragged mustache. "Mr. Jezhek?"

Stone nodded.

"We got your truck ready. Barely. Next time, could you give us more than six hours notice?"

Stone crossed his arms. "You got more notice than I did."

"It was damn hard fabbing alloy panels to match the design your people sent–"

"Do you want more of our work in the future? Lead me to it.

The pudgy man led him through the interior door, down a narrow hallway. The rustle of his roller case's wheels grew louder between the wallboards. The clank of machinery and the slangy voices of young men came from an open space at the end of the hall.

Double-height ceiling, concrete floor, a dozen vehicles torn down into oily metal skeletons and glossy body panels like bits of a giant's body armor. Smells of lubricating oil and new tires. Infrastructure maintaining the civilized world, usually kept well out of Stone's sight.

A squat wheeled robot squirted rubber protectant onto the new tires of an extended cab pickup truck. Stone frowned. Hideously anti-quated design–not the robot, the truck. Rounded lines and not a single straight edge.

Another robot, its football-sized body bobbing on six spidery legs, buffed flexible solar panels covering the truck's hood. Running boards and a black metal cage in front of the radiator grill rounded out the list of the truck's most visible features. If his black coupe were a slot receiver, this truck resembled an offensive lineman, from the days when football players blocked with their bare hands and tackled oppo-nents to the ground.

"We added a fuel cell with a forty-gallon tank," the pudgy man said. "The fuel cell will catalyze any material with carbon and hydrogen you pour in, though the fewer contaminants, the better." He set his hands on his hips and squinted up and down Stone's golf-casual garb. "There's a full set of controls as well. That's steering wheel, shift lever, accelerator–"

"Is it?" Stone's sarcasm filled the space.

The pudgy man blinked, clear sign he believed Mr. Jezhek couldn't drive worth a damn. "Standard transponder-assisted and autonomous driving modes. By switch or by voice commands you can force autonomous mode or override to full manual mode. Get caught using it on public highways and our ass is in a sling same as yours."

"I'll only use it where I won't get caught." Stone paused. "I asked for a custom toolkit."

"We packed everything you asked for. Flip up the bench seat in the back of the cab if you want to check it."

Hell yes he wanted to check. Stone walked around the truck's hulking engine compartment toward the driver's door. There, he pressed his thumb to the lock. His implantable and transcranial stim mesh relayed instructions from the truck's computer to his field of vision. Hold three seconds, stare at a virtual dot superimposed on the door post–the truck's locks snicked open.

Stone pulled open the rear driver's side door, climbed into the thin white illumination of an LED mounted in the ceiling. A loop of tan leather, the same color as the rest of the rear seat, poked out from between the bench and the backrest. He tugged it and the bench seat flipped up. The LED cast sharp shadows onto a mass of tools carefully tucked into slots in slate-gray compressed foam: first aid kit, cable ties of varying lengths, expandable magnetic-resonance helmet for improvised interrogations, a flare gun, a snub-nosed revolver, a handheld rotary cutter, a spool of peel-and-stick transponders to track suspect vehicles or locations....

He nodded to himself. Every expected item and each in its place. If needed, he could find any tool in the dark, or blindfolded, or upside down in a lake with water flooding the cab.

The pudgy man shifted his feet. His tight face suggested heartburn.

Stone stepped onto the running board and spoke over the top of the cab. "Anything else? I'll be off."

Roller case to the front passenger seat, then Stone climbed behind the wheel. The electric motor hummed and the instrument panel lit up.

In front of him, a garage door lifted, showing the service drive behind the building.

He paused and ran his hands over the controls. His fingers bumped over the stitches in the steering wheel's leather. His foot pressed the brake pedal and he shifted from park to drive. The truck lurched once, a hound eager to slip the leash.

Not yet, boy. You'll get your chance on Freeland.

Stone shifted back into park, then reached to the bottom of the steering column for the manual-control switch. He flicked it and the nav computer lit up in the center console. Another computer-generated woman, this one brunette and freckled, with a voice as smooth and bland as unflavored pudding. "Do you wish to set an override code?"

"Yes..." His afternoon with the peewee football players came back to him. "Override code: cornerback."

"Thank you. Destination?"

The Genomics tech's advice came back to him. Better to buy them and not need them than the reverse. "A place that sells condoms. Then take me to the wormhole to Freeland."

CHAPTER 4

Two nighttime hours on the freeway took Stone out of Houston and its suburbs, onto a climb up a rolling plain westbound toward San Antonio. A steady line of robotic tractor-trailers rolled down the right lane, two hundred yards apart. The electric engine of Stone's new truck purred past the tractor-trailers, until the nav computer bonged and the truck slid over for his exit.

A glow from elevated signs lit up fast food joints and refueling stations. Empanadas Del Rey and Taj Mahal Tandoor glared at each other across a state highway. The glow from QuikCharge's sign washed out the asphalt under the blinking yellow light where the state highway intersected the off ramp. In front of the Grab&Go, a scrawny male figure in denim jacket and cowboy hat held the elbow of a pregnant woman waddling to a dented pickup. Rural people living petty lives–

Ten thousand small towns hold more people than all your decadent neighbors on your concrete-covered island. The thought wedged sharp angles into crevices of his mind. *And after Time of Troubles 2.0, those rural people will survive when a terrorist H-bomb vaporizes Manhattan.*

Stone quirked his eyebrow, then subvoked to his implantable, *Tell cover stories they made this one too intrusive.*

Parallel to the ramp, segmented retaining walls held back a giant wedge of dirt curving toward a line of thick concrete pillars climbing toward the interstate. Orange-striped signs and barrels cluttered the road side like garish fungi. A freeway spur to the new wormhole. Once construction was complete, a thousand settlers would take the exit to Freeland every day.

Stone's truck slowed at the end of the ramp, then swung left onto the state highway. Two lanes with a yellow stripe between them and a broad asphalted shoulder. The lights at the freeway intersection faded in the rear view mirror and the rolling plain on either side of the highway grew pallid gray in thin moonlight.

A blue square sign soon came into view. Spotlights revealed its words.

NOW ENTERING UNITED NATIONS INTERSTELLAR TRANSPORT BUREAU RESTRICTED ZONE. ALL VEHICLES SUBJECT TO SEARCH.

The sign left out the remote scans already performed by ITB. The truck sped onward. When curves approached, the truck's headlights illuminated brick farmhouses and steel-walled barns. Up close, though, the buildings showed only dark windows and unlit front porches. The farmers lived somewhere else now, bought out by ITB to further the progress of mankind.

Behind barbed wire fences, fields of wild grass rustled in the breeze. Concrete pylons carried a blue pipe as thick as a man's leg–terabit data cable–parallel to the highway. Rising up toward a curve, Stone's headlights lit up a handmade sign of black spray paint on a bed sheet: a cannon's barrel above the words *come and take it*. A last ineffectual protest against inevitable change.

Stone's gaze drifted past the sign to more wild fields. Another foreign thought bubbled up. *A shame all this ranchland is given over to brush and feral hogs.*

The truck slowed again. The headlights panned across a line of solitary oaks running away from the state highway. Gravel of a side road crunched under the truck's wheels.

Ahead, far beyond the reach of the headlights, a glow lurked behind a tree-lined rise. Stone rested his hands on the locked steering wheel and pulled himself forward in his seat as the truck crested the rise.

A hemisphere of daylight shone in the middle of the Texas night, like a fat half-moon fallen sideways to Earth. About fifty yards across, the hemisphere showed a sky a deeper blue than any sky of Earth. Under the hemisphere, a blue-black asphalt slab ran from side to side, perpendicular to a line of gouged dirt. Shells of distortion rippled the night sky just outside the hemisphere's surface.

In front of Stone, just outside the hemisphere's surface, rose a curved tower, about fifteen yards tall by ten wide and deep. Daylight on the tower's sides showed a metal/carbon nanotube alloy surface with a black matte finish. A deeply recessed set of double doors huddled at ground level. The shells of distortion thickened around the vent near the curved tower's roof, where the air rippled with waste heat from the fusion reactor powering the wormhole's exotic matter equilibrator.

From the top of the equilibrator tower, a black strip, the equilibrator ring, arched to the hemisphere's summit and down the far side. The surface of the equilibrator ring facing the wormhole interior shimmered with coiled blue light, all the way down to the ground. The equilibrator ring continued underground and completed the circle at the equilibrator tower's base buried fifteen yards below ground level. Energies corralled by the equilibrator tower and ring kept the wormhole from collapsing on itself and bursting gamma rays tangential to the tower's long axis.

Having reached the limits of his understanding of wormhole physics, Stone stretched his arm to the truck's windshield, then jutted up his thumb. Slivers of blue sky appeared on either side of his thumb.

A sharp feeling pushed at the corners of his mouth. *Gig 'em!* Some glitch from the Jasper Jezhek persona. Stone shook his eyes and let his mind measure the angle and calculate the distance. Eight hundred meters. The truck rolled along, gravel crunching under the tires. Any moment now–

The truck braked. Light banks came on, flanking the road ten yards ahead. A concrete barrier blocked the right half of the road and a tubular steel gate, the left. The lights silhouetted three men in blue uniforms. Their shoulders held patches showing the UN flag distorted by a wormhole. ITB security. If ITB's undercover operatives were keystone kops, these three were meter maids.

Stone set his hands high on the steering wheel. "Window down," he told his truck.

Two security men fanned out, in front of the truck but clear of its path, and cocked their hips near their shooting hands in the manner of insecure policemen everywhere. The third came to the driver's window. Buzz cut hair, lined face. "Good evening. Identification, please."

"Of course." Stone subvoked to his implantable to transmit Jezhek's ID. "Is something the matter?"

"We don't see too many transits this time of night, Mr... Jezz-heck?"

The sharp angled feeling returned, this time aimed outward. Stone kept his voice calm. "Ye-zhek. Is the wormhole closed? My clearance came through today and I don't want to—" He nodded toward the deep blue hemisphere less than half a mile ahead. "—burn daylight."

"You have an important purpose on Freeland?"

"My organization wants to preserve Czech-American culture. Freeland might be the best place for us."

The security man's mouth twisted in passing. "Good luck with that." His gaze shifted to something low and central in his vision. "You're free to go, Mr. Jezz-heck. Traffic control will request permission to override your truck's autopilot. Do not touch your truck's controls, especially when transiting. Best to shut your eyes when entering and exiting the wormhole." Behind him, the gate lifted. "Good day."

In the truck's dark cab, the nav screen pulsed a red border around text repeating the security man's message. Stone tapped *authorize*.

The truck rolled forward and left, then turned right to avoid another concrete barrier. It serpentined around two more barriers before turning to the right, onto freshly-scraped dirt heaped over a culvert shiny in the truck's headlights. The fresh scrape marked a temporary track, bouncing Stone against the seat belt and the leather seat. The hemisphere of Freeland's deep blue sky grew larger to

Stone's left. He passed under the blue data pipeline raised twenty feet above the ground.

A quarter of the way around the wormhole, the track curved to the left. Stone's headlights panned across a wider, deeper scrape through the land, bedecked with orange-and-white safety signs. Dormant bulldozers and rollers waited for the next day's work. A freeway spur at the beginning of construction, along with the narrow raised berm of a forthcoming bullet train line and a elevated terabit conduit, ran parallel to the track and directly at the pit inside the wormhole. The equilibrator ring arched side to side in front of him.

The truck jolted down packed dirt, onto a short run of concrete in what would become the two Earthbound lanes of the freeway spur. Stone stretched his back as he neared the wormhole perimeter. For a moment, everything in Stone's vision stretched away, as if an invisible giant pulled the truck–and his arms–apart. Red tinged all he saw. A moment later, everything snapped closer together and took on a blue-white glow.

Stone yawned. A far cry from his first transit. How much alarm coursed through him then? Jasper Jezhek might be asked about the experience. Try to remember...

The visual effects faded, but Stone suddenly felt almost twice as heavy. The truck rolled onto the asphalt. Above the wormhole, a scattered handful of bright Texas stars glowed in Freeland's deep blue sky. Ahead, inside the wormhole, the asphalt ramped up mounded dirt. A wall of distortion rippled his view of the road angling down to a rust-brown, rocky field tufted by deep green grass.

His truck climbed the ramp. The whisper of fresh asphalt under the tires switched to the whine of rigid steel road decking. Half his weight suddenly lifted from Stone's shoulders. Objects tinged blue-white pressed on his vision, then everything stretched out and reddened like a sunset before snapping back into place. Fresh asphalt whispered anew.

Stone eased against the leather seat in point-eight-two gees. The truck accelerated down to ground level, then cruised almost half a mile. White reflectors accented the dashed white line down the middle of the roadway. The two lanes merged down to one. Grass whipped by, a lumpy, deep green blur. The engine whined a bit louder as it climbed up a viaduct. Below, a blue-clad security man squinted up, leaning his backside against a concrete barrier at ITB's outbound gate.

In the rear view mirror, the equilibrator ring around the wormhole mouth lay on its side next to a rippling dome of washed out darkness. The tower pointed at him like a partial ruin of a bombed stadium.

The orange light of the planet's sun–a K-type star, if he remembered his astronomy-for-artists class in college–bathed the ground and cast a short shadow ahead of the truck. Conditioned air gushed from the truck's vents. Parallel lines of knee-high wooden stakes marched alongside the road, marking the edges of the soon-to-be-built rail line. The blue terabit conduit seemed to float on slender nanotube pilings eight feet off the ground.

On either side of the transport and communications channels, a plain rolled and climbed toward distant ranges of low hills. Barbed wire fences blocked off square fields of rust-brown flecked deep green a quarter of a mile per side. Brown cattle grazed in camera view of self-leveling robots suspended between pairs of tall off-road tires. *Wonder what genes they engineered into that sprangletop grass* nudged at his thoughts. *And the cattle.*

A blue-black asphalt strip bisected more low hills straight ahead. Beyond the hills, a blotch of gray boxy shapes squatted on the horizon. Freeland's capital, Svoboda City. A narrow river, the Novy Morava, meandered through the city. The viaduct ramped down to the right lane of a two-lane road. Svoboda City disappeared behind the hills.

Stone sniffed out a breath and mirth tightened his cheeks. City? He subvoked and his implantable overlaid a factoid in his vision: population 22,873. A small town, alone near the edge of the human-settled galaxy.

A few thousand pawns against the UN's master players. No doubt who would win.

Jasper Jezhek's thoughts when exiting the freeway back in Texas drained the mirth from Stone's face.

CHAPTER 5

Svoboda City's finest hotel, the Mezihvezdny, could have been plucked from one of a thousand airport access roads on Earth. Inside the automatic front doors, the roller wheels on Stone's suitcase clacked across joints in ceramic tile, and the sound echoed off flimsy wallboard. He inhaled. From the thick scent of floor cleaner, at least the staff cleaned the lobby every day.

Stop. Remember the cover story. Jasper Jezhek entered the promised land. Stone gaped his mouth and craned his neck. He dredged for childhood memories.... his first visit to the apatosaurus exhibit at the American Museum of Natural History. Something so big, walking Earth tens of millions of years ago–

Good enough. Stone turned to his left, to the front desk. Two blondes enough alike to be mother and daughter spoke to each other in low voices.

The older one shook her head at the other. "Not a word–" Her shoulders shifted and she turned a bland smile to Stone. "Are you Mr. Jezhek?"

Stone grinned. "You don't know how good it feels to hear a stranger pronounce my name correctly. But how–?"

"If you lived on Freeland–" The younger woman pushed a strand behind a dainty ear. Clear, taut skin and plush lips, twenty-five at most. "–we would recognize you." The curves of her chest aimed a nametag at him, a pale oval against a maroon blouse: Natalie.

The older woman's brown eyes briefly narrowed and glanced sideways. Her attention returned to Stone. "And you're the only person from Earth with a reservation."

"Mom, I know you have a lot of paperwork with–what happened." Natalie patted the older woman's arm. "I'll check in Mr. Jezhek."

Her mother pressed her lips into a bloodless line. "Enjoy your stay, Mr. Jezhek." She slipped through a door behind the front desk.

Stone smiled at Natalie, then craned his neck around. A cheap ceiling of crumbling drop panels. Furniture extruded from vats of plastic or pressed out of crude steel. A far cry from a nearly complete fossil skeleton seventy-five feet long.

Did they dig up that apatosaurus on your tiny island? Or did some Wall Street whiz kid cash out enough junk bonds to buy it?

Natalie's fingers clacked over a keyboard. "Let's see, we could put you on the second floor–oh, no, make that the third floor."

"What's wrong with second?" Stone asked, knowing the answer.

Her smooth cheeks reddened. She snapped her gaze back to her computer monitor. "It's, well, everything is under control, the police...."

"Police?" He put just enough of a waver in his tone.

Natalie glanced back with wide eyes at the door. She raised a slender index finger to her lips. "Please, quietly. Mom's afraid you'll get the wrong idea if you hear. We're a fine hotel, we're a safe planet–"

Stone reached over the plastic-laminate counter and took her free hand between his. Warm and trembling. "I can tell that just by talking to you. What happened that brought the police?"

The trembling in her hand eased. "Our one previous guest from Earth. Mr. Wu. A travel writer. I checked his blog, he wrote about dozens of sites on Earth and other colonies... I'm babbling."

He patted her hand. Others of Gray's employees did yeoman's work in creating a site and inserting it into the worldweb. "It's okay. Tell me more."

"Two days ago, he went out for a day trip." Stone's implantable popped a factoid into his vision. Freeland, younger than Earth and moonless, had a day fourteen hours long. Dragon left the hotel thirty-two hours ago.

Natalie pulled her hand away from Stone and hugged herself. She turned her eyes to the monitor. Her next words came slow and flat. "He seemed fine when he came back that evening, but yesterday, he never responded to the maid's offer to clean. We opened his room around this time yesterday, and, and... he was stretched out, fully dressed, eyes open, dead."

"Strange beds in strange cities sometimes get people doubting what they're doing and why." Where had that come from? Not the Jezhek persona; the thoughts held the flavor of Stone's own mind. He shrugged.

Natalie's lower lip trembled. She hugged herself tighter. "The police said there was no sign of suicide."

"I'm sure it wasn't foul play."

Natalie's gaze swung back to the monitor. "The police believe it was natural causes."

She knew the truth. Not natural causes. Someone invaded Dragon's room and killed him. But if he'd found intel important enough to kill him over, he would have transmitted it through the wormhole to Gray before reaching the hotel. Right?

"Our bodies are complex systems that can fail in all sorts of ways," Stone said. "Wu, his name? A Chinaman?"

She nodded.

"At least he wasn't one of us."

Natalie sniffled. "He was still a guest." She rubbed her eyes and sniffled again. "I'm sorry, you still need your room. Let's see, 308." She pointed to an electronic pad and a device like a school biology lab's microscope on the counter. "Thumb on the pad, eye to the retina scanner. We have the most advanced security of any hotel on the planet. You won't need a key."

In the elevator, Stone's finger hovered over the 2 button, then touched 3. A mechanical clunk and the car rose. Visiting Dragon's room would only get him noticed. Dragon's killers–or the Svoboda City police–presumably scrubbed the room of evidence.

The elevator dinged. Typical hotel hallway with emergency stairwells at either end. He rolled his suitcase past a humming ice machine and down beige carpet, leaving wheel tracks in the vacuumed nap. He swept his gaze around the space, remembering dinosaur skeletons. Tiny warts of cameras, microphones, and sniffers passed through his line of sight.

At first glance, Room 308 like a hundred other hotel rooms on Earth and a dozen colonies. Bathroom on the right near the door, a closet-like cubby opposite. Plastic, glass, and steel furniture, fabricated on a world of immature forests. A quilt on the bed had a homey, flyover look. A mass-produced artwork showed a rancher, two robots, and a herd of cattle under the local orange sun.

He went past the bed and a desk to the windows, pulled back a corner of sheer curtain. Trees with vertically-grooved trunks and linear deep green leaves spread sweeping branches as high as his window over a crushed granite jogging track. *Live oaks.* On the far, west side of the jogging track the ground sloped down to the river. Three- and four-story buildings on the river's opposite bank peeked through the foliage.

Stone dropped the curtain. Distance and the soft cover of tree canopies reduced the risk of a marksman across the river hitting him, but better to reduce it further.

Besides, he wouldn't complete his assignment looking out the window. He flung his suitcase onto the bed and mused while he hung his few changes of clothes in the closet near the front door. With his thumbprint, he locked his two pistols into the room safe inside the closet wall.

The hotel's security servers held video and audio of Dragon's killers. Maybe they'd held him at gunpoint and told him to stay cool on the walk to his room. No, Dragon's biotelemetry didn't transmit signs of nervousness like elevated heart rate....

Unless his killers dosed him with drugs or hacked his transcranial stimulator to clamp his heart rate into a normal range, sixty or seventy beats per minute.

Stone hung a polo shirt on a hanger. Speculation. Get the evidence first. A man from Earth could easily charm a local girl and access the hotel's security servers. Stone reached for the suitcase, found it empty. He packed so little? He shrugged and slid the suitcase onto the closet floor.

Even though Natalie could be useful, Jasper Jezhek hadn't come to the planet to seduce a local girl. Stone subvoked and dossiers on prominent Freelanders popped into his vision. Lukas Benavides, owner of the planet's biggest fleet of automated trucks. Steve Kovar, the construction company owner targeted by anti-UN graffiti, though a real Jasper Jezhek wouldn't know Kovar's sympathies. Elias Schmied, the planetary government's chief executive, the one with the threatened son. Stone paged through the dossiers by gesturing in the air, and texted them to request meetings by jabbing his finger at virtual *contact* buttons and subvocally dictating to his implantable. *I'm with the Pan-American Czech and Slovak Cultural Preservation Society. Here's a link to our website for you to learn more about us. I'd like your help in rescuing more of our people from a modern Earth out to destroy us...*

Messages sent, he laid back on the bed, knees bent and feet on the floor. His left arm felt heavy. His watch said three a.m. and the angled orange sunlight diffused by the sheer curtains said mid-afternoon. Either way, a good time for a nap...

A bell chimed, louder and louder. Stone blinked himself awake and his implantable stopped inducing the alarm in his auditory nerve. Pale sky outside the window. Local time 0330, a few minutes after sunrise.

A calendar popped up with two appointments. Steve Kovar would meet Stone at his company's office in town at 0600. Late morning. Stone squinted. The rich man who would get richer building roads and housing for ten million of the resettled? What would he gain by meeting Jasper Jezhek?

The other appointment made more sense. Lukas Benavides invited him to his ranch twenty miles west of Svoboda City at 0900. Late afternoon. Stone cracked open a plastic water bottle and a smile lifted the corners of his mouth. Kovar did him a favor. Once Benavides learned about Stone's earlier meeting with Kovar–Stone would tell him, even though he might already know before Stone arrived at his ranch–he'd be more likely to believe Stone's cover story. Chat up Natalie between those times and he'd have a productive day.

After he shaved, showered, and dressed in a long-sleeved shirt and golf pants, Stone held the room safe's door open for a moment. Main pistol under jacket, or the 9mm?

The 9mm. Stone holstered it low on his left calf, pulled down his pants leg, and took the elevator to the lobby. He followed a yeasty aroma, spiced with sausage and bacon, to a breakfast room. A dozen people, mostly gray-haired and wrinkled, sat at alloy and plastic tables. They looked up from paper plates holding pastries stuffed with meat, taking him in. Many turned to one another and whispered. A man with a weathered face opened his mouth, his eyes glinting, apparently ready to speak to Stone. A woman next to him, gray hair pinned up, nudged him and whispered something. The man slunk back and nodded, but his gaze followed Stone to the counter.

Havlichek's Bakery, best kolaches in light years read a sign over a dozen trays of meat-stuffed pastries. Stone pointed and robotic arms jutting from the wall loaded a paper plate with a kolache stuffed with bacon and another with *huevos rancheros*, whatever that might be. He carried his plate to a table near the man with the weathered face.

He took his first bite of the *huevos rancheros* kolache. Scrambled eggs and a diced vegetable, maybe green pepper. The old man said, "I reckon you're the man from Texas."

Not green pepper. A pickled jalapeño burned Stone's mouth. Internally, the Jezhek persona laughed. Stone swallowed, coughed. "That's right." His hand lifted off the table for water, but he'd left the bottle in his room.

"We were born there," the old man said. "Melissa and me both." He extended a liver-spotted hand to his wife. "I was 12 when my parents got tickets for one of the warp-drive ships. Young, but old enough to understand why my dad wanted us to leave."

"Connor," Melissa said, "let this nice young man eat his breakfast."

From under bushy white eyebrows, Connor drilled his gaze into Stone. "Was Earth as bad as he said?" He leaned forward. "Is it still?"

Stone set down the kolache. Connor's questions would give him a break from eating jalapeños. "Sir, I don't know what your father might have said, but my history teachers told me a lot of bad things happened during the Time of Troubles. Ethnic strife nearly destroyed the United States, and wars and terrorism killed billions around the world."

Connor turned to Melissa. "See? You want to believe the best of everyone. I love you for that, but sometimes it's misplaced." Melissa inhaled sharply.

Stone looked away from the marital drama the old couple reenacted. His gaze panned to the doorway and his eyes widened. Natalie stood just inside the breakfast room. Maroon polo and khaki pants clung to her ninety-minute hourglass curves. Her wide brown eyes focused on Stone.

"But Earth must be better now," Melissa said, voice meek. "They can make those tunnels in space." To Stone: "How is Earth now?"

"Ma'am, every licensed journalist on the Worldforum says things are much better than the Time of Troubles."

Connor's mouth curled as he glanced at Melissa. He said to Stone, "You chose your words carefully. What do real people say whose jobs don't depend on telling official lies?"

Stone stiffened, then relaxed his limbs as if noticing Freeland's low gravity for the first time. "I've never been able to speak freely to strangers before. It doesn't come easily."

"How bad is it, son?" Connor asked.

"There's as much crime and ethnic strife as when your families left," Stone said. "It's simply been moved out of the big cities."

Natalie came closer, angling her head toward Stone. Around the breakfast room, the guests paused with kolaches in hand and leaned forward.

Details bubbled up from the Jezhek persona. "I grew up on a ranch outside La Grange. My father remembers ours being a town of less than ten thousand people, mostly folks like us, and even the ones who weren't like us worked and didn't agitate about microaggressions and whatever privilege we supposedly have. But before I was born, the power brokers in Austin and Houston pushed twenty thousand welfare recipients onto us." He shook his head sadly for Melissa's benefit. "And every other small Texas town I ever heard of, except those full of weekend houses for the urban rich."

To the right, a woman with creased forehead and over-rouged cheeks said, "Small-town values could help welfare recipients become productive."

"I wish that were true," Stone said from the Jezhek persona. "But the power brokers kept up the same damned welfare state–pardon my language, ma'am–that ruined the big cities."

More impressions came to mind. Not from the Jezhek persona, but from Stone's memory. Eight or nine, a family reunion at Paw-Paw Chalmers' mansion. An older boy, one of Stone's second cousins, his skin two shades darker than Paw-Paw's and his thirteen-year-old arms already muscled. Hard shoves during the backyard football game, and sneers at the white women among the biracial crowd of grandmothers chatting on the deck. *Which muthafuh'in Becky be yo grandmama?*

"Every crime you can imagine started to happen," Stone said, his voice more intense. "We didn't just have to lock our doors, we had to put up burglar bars and security cameras. Even then, if you go to the police with video showing who broke into your house, they won't do anything. The police claim to be overworked but it's really because the power brokers will investigate them–the police, not the criminals!–for profiling and disparate impact."

Natalie scraped a chair's feet back from an empty table and sat. All the guests in the room stared his way while their kolaches sat uneaten in front of them.

The Jezhek persona pushed more details at Stone. "More crimes, and worse, than that take place. Vandals shoot cattle in the belly and leave them to die. Hasn't happened to my family, but only because the welfare recipients are too lazy to drive far from their subdivisions. Robberies in broad daylight. Two fatal stabbings at the biergarten. A high school girl dragged into the boy's restroom between classes and–" He looked away from the women in the room. "–dishonored. After that, our kind of people pulled our children out to homeschool. You know what happened then? Inspectors from 'Child Protective Services," Stone said, his air-quoting fingers curling as much as his sneering lips, "most of whom should be back on welfare, come out to investigate our people–us!–for homeschooling. So our choices are bribe the inspectors, face jail time and lose our children to foster care, or send our children into jungle schools."

Connor, face drained of color, slowly shook his head. "God help us." Men and women around him nodded.

"He did," Stone said. Eyebrows crinkled, and every gaze on him became even more intent. "He gave us the wormhole that hundreds of thousands of our people can use to join you here."

The hotel guests all nodded. Natalie held her head rigid, an expression he read as appraising him.

His face firm, his eyes clear, Stone nodded at her, then swept his gaze across the room. Poor fools, thinking a hundred thousand of their co-ethnics could stand against the clamoring millions soon to come through the wormhole from ten thousand shantytowns. The power brokers–and not those in provincial cities like Austin and Houston, but the true masters of the human galaxy–would win, and only a fool would resist them.

The only person in the room not a fool was him.

CHAPTER 6

At the western edge of Svoboda City, behind a wire-mesh fence eight feet high, Steve Kovar's office building partially blocked the view of an equipment yard. Stone's truck pulled up at a portable, automated gatehouse, its paint glossy and unworn. A screen with a virtual security guard halted him until he spelled J-e-z-h-e-k. The gate slowly lifted for him to pass, then clanged shut a foot behind his back bumper.

Stone parked in front of the building but he managed a glimpse of heavy construction equipment on his way to the door. Gigantic tires compressed the gravel under a flatbed truck, near a dormant backhoe and bulldozer. Clangs slipped under the closed door of a corrugated steel building in the corner of the equipment yard. Cows–*cattle*, the Jezhek persona corrected–grazed on the far side of the fence, on fields that ran to the low hills to north and south. Fields which the backhoe and bulldozer would soon cover with housing for ten million of the resettled.

Chilled air spilled out of the front door. A receptionist, a young woman barely more than a girl, with lank hair and plain features, guided Stone to a corner office on the upper floor. "Dad, Mr. Jezhek is here."

"Thanks, hon." His daughter withdrew. Kovar waddled on stumpy legs around a wood-grain plastic desk glowing with embedded touchscreens. Thinning brown hair, plump cheeks, and a double chin showed his age and appetite. His belly pushed out a short-sleeved, pastel yellow buttoned shirt with his company name in red on the left breast. His hand pillowed around Stone's. Soft brown eyes studied Stone's face. "Mr. Jezhek, I'm truly honored, you've come all the way from Earth and want to talk to me."

"It's not far at all, anymore," Stone said.

Jezhek's adam's apple bulged and bobbed. "Very true, very true. All my life Earth has been impossibly far away. A place my parents talk about. And now here you are. Takes some getting used to."

"For me, too, to be here. I appreciate your time and don't want to waste it. Perhaps we could sit?"

"Yeah, yeah, of course. A drink? Coffee?"

"Just water."

Kovar nodded and tapped the company name on his shirt. "Hon, bring us a water and... water."

His daughter's voice came through speakers hidden in the ceiling. "No coffee, dad?"

"No, no, I drank enough already this morning." Kovar tapped the company name on his shirt, closing the connection, then met Stone's gaze and pointed at a round table and two cloth-covered chairs. Stone sat. Thirty inches in diameter and made of the same wood-grain plastic as the desk, the table held a single item: a framed photograph of several girls of sixteen or seventeen, his daughter among them, in pink and purple prom dresses, roses of coordinating color in corsages round their wrist.

"She's very pretty. You must be proud."

Kovar's mouth hung open and he blinked twice. "Oh, oh, yes. I'm a lucky dad. A year out of high school and she's already a big help around here." He wiped the vein-thick back of his hand across his smooth forehead. A hint of sweat remained in the air.

Stone made a mental note of Kovar's reaction. A knock at the door heralded the girl's arrival. She set down a tray bearing a pitcher of ice water and two glasses, poured. Stone's eyes met hers. Her plain features, and what they hinted of the mind behind them, lacked anything to catch his attention. He gave her a weak smile. She lowered her gaze and left the room.

"Thanks again for taking the time to meet me, Mr. Kovar."

"Call me Steve," Kovar said. "We're our own planet but we're also a small town. No need to be formal."

"I understand. Call me Jasper."

"Jasper. So how can I help you?"

"I represent a society that seeks to preserve Czech, especially Texas Czech, culture. As soon as the society heard about Freeland, they wanted to send me here to see if there's room on your planet for us."

After a loud exhalation, Kovar said, "When it comes to room, we've got plenty." He waved a flabby arm at the windows, indicating the miles of ranchland between his equipment yard and the hills. "And we would love to have more of our people come here. You do know about the ancestry requirement for permanent settlers?"

"We do."

"That's acceptable to you?"

Stone dipped his head, then nodded. "Our society's membership is open to anyone with one Czech or Slovak great-grandparent. That's a lower bar than you set here, so some of our members might be barred from joining you here."

Kovar winced, like a salesman trying to sweep away bad news. "That's unfortunate."

"We respect your right as founders to set your rules."

Kovar stroked his fingers along his chin. "We might be able to revisit our ancestry requirement. I'll talk to the chief executive and the important legislators. If our laws are unjust–"

"Don't change them on our account," Stone said. "We aren't like most of the world. We don't feel entitled to get a break because we're special snowflakes." His fingers closed on a glass slick with condensation. Ice tinkled as he sipped. "Those of us who could come are mostly ranchers. All we ask for is a fair deal on land to build houses and ranches."

"If you're willing to work hard seeding biomes, you'll get a fair deal. But it will be hard work indeed." Kovar glanced over his shoulder. Stone's gaze followed, settling on eight, no, nine brown cows–cattle–half a mile to the west. The cattle's heads bowed to nibble the deep green grass.

Half-remembered facts from school science classes came to Stone. On ninety percent of extrasolar planets bearing life, evolution had failed to bring plants or animals from out of the sea. "This continent was lifeless when your ships arrived?"

Kovar nodded. "The oceans teem with single-cell photosynthetic organisms. The founders debarked from their ships and immediately breathed the air. But the native life never evolved into animals or land plants. Is that common around the galaxy?"

"Very common. We understand the work it would take. Work your parents and your generation have already done." Stone gestured at the windows. "Grinding up the rocky surface, mixing with water and a sludge of microorganisms, then seeding successive waves of more advanced plant and insect life before we could even think about grazing cattle. We understand, and we would gladly do it..." Stone set his face into a haggard look. "...to get away from the ruin the UN inflicted on Texas."

A squint made Kovar's small eyes even tinier. "It's really that bad?"

"Yep."

"Only in spots, right?"

Stone shook his head. "Bad enough all over to get tens of thousands of our people clamoring to leave."

Kovar ducked his head to his glass, then hid his mouth by taking a drink.

"I know it's tough to imagine," Stone said. "The people who run Earth selling out the people who keep human civilization running to win votes from barbarians. But it's true."

Kovar's adam's apple bobbed. "I, I had no idea."

"Now you do. It's what motivates us, Steve. Our people need clear skies and open land to build a better life. Which brings me to the last bit of help I have to ask for."

Kovar dabbed his brow with the back of his hand. "Yes?"

"Don't take their blood money."

"Blood money? Whose money?"

"The UN follows a standard procedure when a colony joins the Dubai Convention. It auctions off the resettlement of tens of millions of undesirables from whichever UN member government spends the most political capital. To get a colony to take those tens of millions, the UN buys off the colony's movers and shakers. Not usually with bribes. Mostly with fat contracts for infrastructure. A lot of rich people and power brokers on a lot of colonies will sell out their own people for solar-electric Mercedes sedans and shopping trips to Park Avenue and Rodeo Drive." Stone bored his gaze into Kovar's beady eyes, and lied. "I can tell you won't sell out Freeland."

Kovar's jaw ground behind his thick face. "'Undesirables?' What does that mean?"

"It means any people a government wants to exile from its territory. Ethnic and religious minorities and political opponents are common targets. Countries where sex selection technologies are commonly used ship out millions of excess young men. Sometimes criminals and welfare recipients get resettled so a government can improve its balance sheet." Stone glanced at the photo of teenage girls in prom dresses. "Mostly men you want nowhere around these pretty young ladies."

Kovar's head jerked down and to the side. Under wide eyebrows, his gaze tightly spiraled around his daughter. Still looking at the photo, he said, "I suspected the UN's offer had strings attached."

"Has the UN approached you already with infrastructure contracts?"

"No, no." He wrenched his gaze away from the photo. "And I assure you, Jasper, I won't pave the way for any undesirables to come here."

Kovar could lie as easily as Stone, it seemed. Or had the threats against him and planetary executive Schmied cowed him?

Pudgy fool. He had more to fear from the UN than a few disgruntled locals.

"I'm glad to hear that. You're busy, so I won't take any more of your time. I'll write up a formal proposal of how much land and equipment we'd like you to donate to us, and send it after I get back to Earth."

"Yes, yes, looking forward to it." Kovar stood and Stone mirrored him. Kovar extended his soft hand. Sweat now clammed his palm. He pulled his hand away and touched the company name on his polo shirt. "Hon, would you show Jasper out?"

"Sure." A moment later, the door swung open. Kovar's daughter beckoned for Stone to follow her into the hallway.

As he left, Stone glanced back through the open door. Kovar stood near the small table, eyes turned to the photograph of his daughter and her friends.

The route back to the hotel followed a wide, divided street, Blaha Boulevard, lined with live oaks. On side streets to the right, behind bakeries and biergartens lining the avenue, extruded plastic tricycles and baseball tees cluttered the yards of one-story houses faced in stone blocks and roofed by corrugated steel. On the left, stacked cubes of plate glass and sinuous alloy raised UN flags above a church's steeple. Offices and residences for ITB and other UN agencies preparing the colony for the coming influx of the resettled. A breeze tugged at the flags' ends but failed to unfurl them as Stone's truck hummed by.

Down one side street, men in orange vests and hard hats trudged around capped-off pipes and conduits poking from a quarter-acre of scraped dirt. A sign read *Another project of Kovar Construction.*

The truck drove on, rigid steering wheel disconnected from the wheels. Motion in the rear-view mirror caught Stone's gaze. A low sedan with faceted surfaces, pale green with a UN employee license plate, turned from a side street and followed him toward the riverfront.

The pale green sedan waited behind his truck at a traffic light. It looked like a stealth aircraft in contrast to the sweeping curved lines of his truck and local vehicles. He checked the mirror again. Through the front window's tint he made the outline of bucket seats spun round to face the cabin. No sign of a passenger.

After the light turned green, his gaze repeatedly darted to the mirror like a tongue to an aching tooth. Still no indication of who might be riding in the sedan. At Novy Morava Avenue, his truck turned right toward his hotel. The pale green sedan crossed his rear view mirror, heading up City Bridge to cross the river.

Stone blew out a breath. The truck turned off the street and pulled up in front of the Mezihvezdny. He went in while his vehicle drove off to park.

Natalie looked up from the front desk. Her lips parted and a glint formed in her brown eyes. "How are you, Mr. Jezhek?"

"Call me Jasper. I'm doing great, thanks. I just had a productive meeting with Steve Kovar."

Her brow crinkled. "Productive? With him?"

"You look surprised."

"I overheard what you said. This morning. In the breakfast room—"

"I saw you there." Stone angled his head. Accessing the hotel's security recordings would require her help. "It cheered me up to see you after all the sad things I talked about. But where does the surprise come from?"

"Because Kovar—" Natalie shifted her gaze to the monitor. "Some people say he wants Earth to dump welfare recipients on us."

"Really? I didn't get that impression. He told me he wants to do what's best for our people, both here and on Earth."

She looked up and rotated her wrist a quarter-turn, a gesture like a shrug. "Maybe people said what they said without knowing what Kovar really wants." Her tone hung in the air, like a musical phrase waiting for the proper closing note.

"Or he lied to me?"

Her voice crept over the counter. "Or maybe he changed his mind."

Poor girl, unwilling to question the motives of Freeland's rich and powerful. The coming tidal wave of ten million resettled would wash her up far from home, if it didn't rip her out to sea. "He at least listened to what I had to say. Hopefully Mr. Benavides will do as much this afternoon."

Natalie perked up. "Lukas Benavides? He'll do that for you, and more. You can trust him to want the best for all our people."

"You've given me even more to look forward to in meeting him." Stone rested his forearms on the counter and leaned toward her. "Maybe I can tell you about it after I get back tonight?"

Red tinged her cheeks. She tucked blond strands behind her ear. "I'll be working tonight."

"All night?"

Natalie smiled at him. She soon turned away, but the smile lingered on her lips. "We can talk more after you get back."

"Till then." He pushed off the counter and went to the elevator. In his room, he ordered lunch, a cardboard tray containing a hamburger and fries from a nearby delivery restaurant. Fluffy, hot fries, and beef and tomato flavors flooded his mouth.

Almost as good as a hot dog with kimchi from the cart near his apartment.

He held his finger to the disposal button on the tray's side. Three seconds later, the cardboard folded in on itself. The tray's seams popped as it compressed into a lump the size of a squash ball. Stone tossed the lump into the recycling can by the door, then went back downstairs.

Behind the counter, deep vertical creases and gray hairs marked Natalie's mother. She turned to Stone and gasped in a breath. Face frozen, only her eyes moved toward the cowboy-styled plastic chairs in the lobby sitting area.

A woman in a dark blue pantsuit unfolded lean legs and rose to about the height of his chin. Sandy blond hair parted straight down the middle spilled over her shoulders. Her jacket lapels and shirt collar splayed wide, exposing her lean neck in the latest New York fashion. A clip held a UN employee's badge to her jacket pocket.

She narrowed large hazel eyes up at Stone, plainly an effort to be taken seriously. "Mr. Jezz-heck?"

He stopped with his feet wider than his shoulders. Hands in pockets, thumbs out. "Yezh-ek," he drawled.

"My name is Caitlyn Fredriksen. I'm with ITB Public Affairs." Her hazel eyes narrowed further. "You and I are going to talk."

CHAPTER 7

Fredriksen led Stone into the parking lot. He squinted at the cloudless sky and she slipped on sunglasses, fingernails glistening with transparent polish. A steady stream of cars and trucks whizzed by on the street and the pavement heated Stone's feet through the treaded soles of his lace-up shoes.

The pale green sedan popped its left-side doors for them. "Inside," Fredriksen said.

"Where are you taking me?"

"Nowhere. Inside the car is the most secure place we can talk."

On the far side of Novy Morava Avenue, between two of a line of potted live oaks, a strolling couple window-shopped at a jewelry store. Vehicles cruised along as if their passengers ignored the two people from Earth. "Seems secure enough right here."

She turned on him and crossed her arms. "Get inside the car or ITB will raid PACSCuPS' offices on suspicion of making willful false statements to a UN agency."

The sky looked a smidgen brighter. PACSCuPS? His cover organization. Knowing Gray, a dozen people worked in an Austin office with the Society's logo on the door... but ITB would plumb the depths of Gray's ruse before Stone returned to Earth.

He shrugged and climbed in, sat on the rear bench, feet on the carpeted floor and hands flat on his thighs. Fredriksen crossed her legs in one of the reversed bucket seats facing him. The tinted windshield and windows tinged the outside a dull brown. The door locks thunked. Cheap plastic upholstered a thin cushion under his backside and an artificial flowery smell of carpet shampoo overwhelmed his nose. He raised his eyebrow and a smirk trickled into his mouth.

Fredriksen's hazel eyes shifted focus into the air between them. "You requested an expedited transit clearance for the purpose of 'establishing ties with fellow members of a cultural minority.'" She narrowed her eyes and arched a light brown eyebrow. "Do you have a response?"

"You didn't ask a question." The smirk flowed into the corner of his eyes.

"Did you state that in your request for expedited processing?"

"I can't remember the exact words. Why do I need to? You're obviously reading the request while we're talking. If you're quoting me accurately, then, yes, that's what I said."

"But establishing ties is not your purpose here."

Stone folded his arms and tilted his head back to peer down his nose at her. "I know my purpose here better than you do."

Fredriksen returned an unflinching look. "Is your purpose denigrating the UN and the Dubai Convention?"

A cold nodule bloomed inside his chest. Stone blanked his face. Who talked? One of the hotel guests in the breakfast room? Natalie? Kovar? Or did she fish for incriminating evidence?

The cold nodule extended into his belly. Not a Public Affairs bureaucrat. He sat across from a keyhole kop. His gaze skimmed the outlines of her pantsuit jacket for a hidden pistol, didn't find it. He met her gaze. "No."

"Took you a while to think about your answer, didn't it?"

Stone dabbed his tongue between parted lips. "An ITB official threatened my employer. I got nervous."

"Did you now?" Fredriksen peered at Stone. Despite her high cheekbones and large eyes, her expression communicated authority.

Not bad for a keyhole kop. He swallowed, continuing the act of Jezhek's nervousness.

"Let's assume for now you're telling me the truth, Mr. Yezh-ek. It would greatly complicate my job if you were not."

The authoritative edge fled from her expression. A Public Affairs bureaucrat after all? "God forbid I complicate your job."

She blinked her large hazel eyes. "I'm here to help the locals see the benefits of the Dubai Convention."

"Benefits? Like all the 'benefits' the Dubai Convention inflicted on the original colonists of Mishima-no-sekai and Nova Santa Catarina?"

"Oh? You've visited Mishima-no-sekai?" She sweetened her voice around the barb.

Stone glared at the space where her wearable projected his file. "You already know the answer."

"I do, but let's make it clear for the record."

He forced the word out of his mouth. "No."

"Nova Santa Catarina?"

He watched his hands wiping on his thighs. "Never been there either."

"So you know nothing about intercommunity affairs on either world?"

"Rumors spread despite the worldweb."

"Or *to* spite it." Fredriksen's plush lips formed a cold smile. "So I can conclude that if the Freelanders hear from you horror stories about the Convention, you would be idly speculating? Or lying?"

"You'll conclude what you want," Stone said. "Regardless of the truth."

"Based solely on the truth. Mr. Yezh-ek, you're free to establish as many ties with the Freelanders as you can. But if you make my job harder, with idle speculation or with lies, ITB security will hustle you back through the wormhole and you will never return. You or any member of the PACSCuPS. Ever. Do you understand me?"

"I understand." He jammed his hands into his pockets. His right index finger probed the pocket's bottom seam. *There.* "Don't worry, I won't tell the cattle that the chute leads them to the slaughterhouse."

Fredriksen shook her head like a teacher in a classroom of undisciplined students. "Do remember what I said about idle speculation, Mr. Yezh-ek." The door locks thunked open. "Good day."

Stone pulled his hands out. A microthin texture, sticky and papery, clung to his right index finger. He climbed out of the car and shoved the door closed with his right hand. He squinted against the orange sunlight and the pale green sedan slipped out of the parking spot. The tires whispered over asphalt, then turned right, toward Blaha Boulevard.

He subvoked a command to his implantable, then wiped a faint adhesive residue off his finger and onto his cargo pants. A map of the city popped into a corner of his vision. A yellow dot turned left on Blaha Boulevard, heading toward the UN quarter.

If he saw Caitlyn Fredriksen coming, she would never get in his way again.

The orange sun hung almost halfway down the western sky. His head jolted, widening his eyes. Stone shook his watch past his cuff. Already 0815.

Tell the truck to drive up, he subvoked. Sweat dabbed the back of his shirt. From around the corner of the hotel, a bulky white shape entered the corner of his vision. It slid up in front of him and opened the driver's door. He lifted a foot to the running board and cool air spilled over him.

Time to visit Lukas Benavides.

The City Bridge arced over the river's sandy islands and meandering main channel. Stone's truck followed Blaha Boulevard through a light industrial quarter. A brewery exuded a thick sweet smell that wormed into the cabin and Stone's nose. Another reason not to drink.

The truck turned southeast, onto Frichville Highway, a broad street of gray asphalt flanked by steel sheds, storage tanks, cooling towers. A worse stench than beer soon dominated the street. Manure. Concrete pillars raised a stockyard's corrugated metal roof above a narrow maze lined with red metal bars. Further back from the street, screened by the stockyard and, behind it, a line of drooping oaks, stood a slaughterhouse.

Stone sniffed. The stockyard's manure taint overwhelmed any stink of blood and raw meat.

Sheds and tanks lining the road thinned out. The road narrowed to two lanes, the shoulders' edges crumbling and purple tar splotching repaired potholes like second-rate facelifts. The last buildings fell behind him. Cattle grazed behind barbed wire fences, oblivious of his truck, oblivious of everything but the sprangletop grass mashed between their jaws. A green sign announced *Frichville 104 Hornik City 193*.

Over a hundred miles of nothing? His shoulders hunched. Stone jabbed the climate control button to raise the truck cab's temperature.

The plain rolled three directions to the horizon and solitary clouds tumbled across the sky. Svoboda City mottled the plain in the rear-view mirrors, a small town growing tiny, and soon, after the road crested and descended a rise, vanishing from sight.

He rode along the thin asphalt ribbon between miles of fields. Empty land under an immensity of sky... Stone raised the temperature another degree.

The truck slowed. Stone let out a long breath. A smaller road ran from Frichville Highway off to the left. The truck turned onto gritty asphalt. The road's shoulders ended two feet outside faded white stripes. Both the nav display in the truck's console and a sign at the roadside warned *Transponder-Assisted Zone Ends 1/4 Mile. Full Automatic or Manual Driving Modes Only*.

Stone rested his hands on the locked steering wheel. His right foot settled on the accelerator pedal, also locked in place. The truck passed a sign marking the end of the transponder-assisted zone. A green tell-tale in the instrument cluster showed the truck switched to automatic mode.

Forget that. "Manual override," Stone said. Warning lights flashed in the nav display and the wheel became a live thing under his grip. The engine slowed and Stone pressed the pedal. Acceleration nudged him deeper into the seat. A grin creased his mouth. Gentle corrections by his hands kept the truck on course through gentle turns. His grin widened.

Empty planets held one advantage over Manhattan.

The pavement gave way to gravel, two lanes wide and graded toward the drainage ditches. The rear wheels touched gravel and slewed. Stone effortlessly straightened the truck's course and kept on. Other than the overlapping tracks of wide tires, faintly visible as smoother strips in the gravel, the gravel road might not have seen traffic in weeks.

More barbed wire, more grazing cattle on either side. A jagged line of dwarf live oaks followed a gully. A steel culvert under the gravel carried the gully under the road. Where was–?

The nav display pinged. Obelisks of stone block came into view on the right. Stone slowed the truck and turned between the pillars. A reversed B in a circle flashed by on the obelisks' faces. The truck's tires rattled over steel tubes laid across a trench dug from pillar to pillar.

It's called a cattle guard came from the Jezhek persona.

More gravel popped under the tires. A half-mile ahead up a mild slope, Benavides' ranch house showed a low silhouette against the deep blue sky.

Svoboda City would feel like Manhattan when Stone returned to the hotel.

Near the ranch house, the gravel driveway forked. One branch looped close to the front door and around a solitary live oak nearly as tall as the ones outside his hotel room. The driveway's other branch curved past the house, over the crest of the slope, and down to a cluster of corrugated metal buildings, two stories high, near a fenced-in field.

Disguised as roadside rocks and galls on the live oak's trunk, microphones and cameras leaped out to Stone's trained eye.

Stone turned onto the loop toward the ranch house before the Jezhek persona could rattle off which farm work took place in which barn. He parked the truck between the live oak and the front door, climbed out. A breeze rustled the live oak's canopy and tumbled a leaf toward his feet. Wood smoke and spices came to his nose.

Shoes crunching gravel, he went around the truck toward a path of granite slabs leading to the ranch house. The house sprawled along the terrain, faced in tan brick and roofed by clay-red, rippled sheet metal.

Brick pillars lined a breezeway along the front of the house, where stood a thick wooden door.

A man with skin the shade of creamed coffee strode on black cowboy boots toward Stone. Horizontal lines–brim of black cowboy hat, stern black eyebrows, narrowed brown eyes, thick gray mustache–transected his lean head. He stopped in front of Stone and dipped his chin once. "I'm Luke Benavides."

"Jasper Jezhek."

Benavides extended his hand. "*Jak se máš?*"

The persona translated *how are you?* and pushed a stiff reply through Stone's mouth. *Je mi dobře, děkuji. A ty?"* I am well, thank you. And you?

Stone shook hands. Benavides squeezed his grip. "You don't speak much Czech."

"I took two years of it at A&M and forgot almost everything. None of us speak it day-to-day any more."

"Not much cause to use it here either, I'm afraid," Benavides said. From the back of the house sounded indistinct voices, a young woman and an older man. He glanced that direction. A puff of white smoke showed over the roof.

Benavides put his hand on Stone's shoulder. "Come inside. We've got a lot to talk about, and we'd like you to stay for dinner."

CHAPTER 8

Benavides led Stone into a spacious room paneled and beamed in honey-colored synthetic wood. A fireplace of mortared rock divided the room in half. A bull's preserved head glared down from its mount above the mantle. Squat couches and chairs covered in tan leather and nailhead trim dominated the part of the room nearest the front door, and a long dining table, slab top and chunky legs of a darker synthetic wood, showed its ends on either side of the fireplace.

He hung his black hat on a rack near the door, then waved at the nearby couch. "Have a seat, Mr. Jezhek."

"Jasper, please."

Benavides nodded, approving. "Luke. A drink, son?"

Stone sat on leather softened by age. "Iced tea. Unsweet."

"You sure? We've got plenty of beer and wine."

A clammy feeling ran down Stone's neck and upper chest. A little truth wouldn't hurt. "My father drank himself into an early grave."

"That's a damn shame. Unsweet tea, coming up." Benavides pulled a small tablet computer from his back pocket and murmured into it. "Should be here soon." His cowboy boots clomped across the synthetic wood flooring to a chair facing Stone. He lowered himself into the chair and slid the tablet onto a side table. "Tell me about yourself, son. A&M, you said. I'm an Aggie too, class of '57."

Stone blinked. About a century old, yet Benavides remained very vigorous. Uncommon enough on Earth, where every major country had thousands of longevity doctors. How many doctors immigrated here on the warp drive ships?

For a moment, the slits of Benavides' eyes narrowed further, but the expression soon eased. "Tell me more about A&M these days."

"I graduated over fifteen years ago."

"You look young for your age. Do you go back for homecoming?"

Memories of alumni days in Greenwich Village bubbled up... and the Jezhek persona clamped down on them. Stone slowly shook his head. "I'm sure a lot has changed since your Old Army days, but an Aggie remains welcome back on campus every day. We still leave homecoming for the tea-sips."

Benavides raised his thick eyebrows. "Tea-sip? I haven't heard anyone call a Texas student that since I was a student. No, before I was a student."

"Our forefathers did some things right. Right enough we should bring those things back."

"Well said, son. Now where the hell are those drinks?" Benavides yanked the tablet off the table with a scrape and growled into it.

After he set the tablet back down, Stone said, "I'd like to hear more about how you came to Freeland."

"You mean, why did Texas Czechs let a Messican on their ship?" Benavides barked out a laugh. "I don't blame you for asking." His expression darkened. "The way the crime and disorder trends were going when we left, I don't blame you for asking at all."

"I'd simply like to know the stories of our Freelander cousins."

"You're polite, but son, between us, we're going to call an entrenching tool a spade. Agreed?"

Stone nodded.

"My father's side of my family lived in Texas for two hundred and fifty years," Benavides said. "One of my forefathers fought in the War of Independence."

Stone blinked. Subtracting 250 from 2060 didn't get to 1776–

Texas *independence* elbowed into Stone's consciousness.

"–helped Sam Houston catch Santa Ana taking a siesta," Benavides said. "I get my Czech ancestry from my mother's side. Her maiden name was Nemec, and her mother's maiden name was a German name, Wendt. Now, son, tell me about your people."

A slow inhalation gave the Jezhek persona time to feed Stone details. A few names of families and small towns, local color about dance halls and high school football games. Stone eyed Benavides and edged his right hand toward his left ankle. If cover stories branch hadn't accounted for a man who might know where Jezhek supposedly came from, the 9mm held a dozen rounds–

"I don't know La Grange," Benavides said, "but sounds like it had a lot in common with my home town." Noises clanked in the distance, behind the dining area on the other side of the fireplace. "Finally."

Boots clomped in the dining area, and around the fireplace came a young woman. Blond hair pulled back from an intelligent face that somehow looked familiar. A dusty denim shirt and matching jeans clung to her long curves. Dried mud clung to the edges of her boots. Her thumb and first two fingers cradled the lip of a beer bottle in her right hand.

Stone stood, barely exceeding the young woman's height. She handed the bottle to Benavides. "Here you go, Deda." Her voice, though as deep as her height suggested, flowed musically.

"Took you long enough," Benavides said, his scolding tone clearly playful.

"Lot of work to do out back," she said, standing in profile to Stone. "And I checked on Uncle Thomas' brisket. Almost done."

"Good. We've got hungry men here."

Silence fell. They shared a glance and Benavides nodded his head a few millimeters.

"A hungry woman too." She turned her shoulders toward Stone. "Mr. Jezhek?"

"Call me Jasper."

Benavides said, "My youngest granddaughter, Teresa."

"*Jak se máš?*" she asked, jutting out her right hand. Her skin proved callused yet warm in Stone's grip.

Confidence filled his eyes. "*Je mi dobře.*"

Teresa withdrew her hand and Stone's breath caught. A pale scrape angled across his palm.

Her plush lips formed an O. "Did I scratch you? Must have bent a nail out back. Sorry."

Stone waved his hand at the air, batting away his discomfort. Confidence returned, edged into a smirk. "You could hurt somebody with those."

"Only if he deserves it. Oh, your tea." Teresa lifted the glass to him. He touched it but she gripped it until his gaze held hers for a moment.

She turned to her grandfather. "Jasper, Deda, pardon me, I should wash up before dinner."

"Don't take too long," Benavides said. His voice took on the playfully scolding tone. "We have important matters to discuss."

The dining table could feed a small army, but only four took seats at the honey-colored synthwood slab. Benavides sat at the head, in a chair tall and solid as befitted a *deda*–grandfather. Behind him, on the other side of picture windows, shadows crept across gray steel barns and an airborne drone hovered and darted like a giant dragonfly. In the distance, brown cattle dissolved into deepening twilight. Hidden speakers softly played piano-and-fiddle polkas under tenors signing in Czech. The Jezhek persona picked out words here and there, *old blacksmith* and *ghost*.

Ten minutes after her departure, Teresa flowed into the chair to Benavides' right, opposite Stone. She could have live theater training, from how much her appearance transformed. Her blond hair hung loosely to the bateau collar of a silky blue shirt, and she looked even more energetic and intelligent than earlier. Touches of makeup, no doubt. The shirt's silky blue matched her eyes.

"Took you long enough," Benavides said.

"Leave a lady her mysteries, Deda." Teresa's chin dipped in a faint nod and she stared at her grandfather for a long moment. Her posture revealed a pair of flesh-tone patches on either side of her long neck, high under her jaw. Subvocal electrodes. Nowhere near as discreet as Stone's transcranial stim network laced around his hair follicles.

Hair. The reason she looked familiar snapped wide Stone's eyes. She'd posed with the other girls in the photo in Kovar's office.

The tenors' next song mingled in some German words. Something about love and sharp and sleep.

The fourth person in the room sat to Stone's left. A broad-shouldered man, wavy salt-and-pepper hair, eyes like brown pebbles. The scent of wood smoke clung to his denim shirt. He coughed against his upper arm and with a parched voice introduced himself as Thomas Benavides, the older man's son and Teresa's uncle.

A robotic cart rolled in from the next room. Its flat top bore serving dishes of potato salad, cole slaw, baked beans, and thick white bread flecked green with jalapeño chunks, along with a carving board holding a thick slab of brisket brown and glistening with crusted spices and melted fat. Stone's mouth watered. The cart popped up a knife on an articulated arm and sliced the brisket. Pieces of fat-veined beef fell sideways, showing off thick pink smoke rings.

Teresa reached for Stone's plate. "You're our guest, Jasper. What would you like?"

The fireplace behind him seemed to concentrate the aromas in the dining room. "Everything." He handed her his plate.

Once steaming plates lay before everyone, Benavides picked up his fork. Stone did the same, hefting chunky stainless steel. A slice of brisket parted effortlessly under his knife and proved perfectly tender when he chewed the first bite. Cut another piece, jab it with his fork–

"You don't get barbecue very often, do you, son?" Crinkles deepened at the corners of Benavides' eyes. The older man idly rotated his beer bottle against the tabletop.

Stone shook his head. "I wish I did."

"Reason enough to make me glad I left Earth." The crinkles faded. "Though I'm sure there are many others, and stronger." Benavides raised his bottle to his mouth.

The Jezhek persona grew stronger within Stone's throat. "You wouldn't recognize Texas anymore." His gaze rested on the condensation ring Benavides' beer bottle left on the synthetic tabletop. Memories came up from the persona, different from the ones deployed that morning to the hotel guests. "Shiner Bock is no longer on sale."

Benavides' face grew a shade paler. "How could the UN stop that?"

"I don't know if the UN, the US government, or the billionaires in the big cities were behind it. It happened before my time. My father told me the power brokers ordered the brewery to make malt liquor and premixed tomato-clam-beer cocktails for the people relocated from the cities into welfare housing in our towns, or else they'd unleash state and federal health, environment, and employment opportunity bureaucrats on them. The brewery didn't have a choice but to comply."

Hell, that story might even be true.

Teresa's fork clattered against her plate. "There's always a choice," she said. Overhead lights cast a warm glow on her features.

Stone nodded. "You think they could quit and start a new brewery?"

Scowling, Benavides shook his head. "Not if the brewery employees wanted to keep their jobs."

Teresa arched a thin blond eyebrow. "Why couldn't they?"

"If their new business stayed small, they might avoid notice. For a while. But eventually they'd end up in the power brokers' gunsights." Stone kept his gaze on her face while he sliced and ate another forkful of brisket.

She matched his gaze for a while, then shrugged. "You know Earth better than any of us."

"Sounds like Earth is just as we suspected," Benavides said.

To Stone's left, Thomas slowly nodded. Stone had almost forgotten his presence. "Yup."

"That's a sad story, Jasper," Teresa said. "And I'm sure you could tell us a hundred more. But Earth doesn't matter, at least not to Uncle Thomas and me. Deda–" She winced at Benavides. "–I know you don't want to hear that–"

"I was born there. I won't die there. I agree with you about what matters to us more than Earth." Benavides turned to Stone. "What happens to human worlds that join the Dubai Convention?"

"That's an interesting question. Before I drove out here from Svoboda City, a UN bureaucrat asked me the same thing."

Forks, knives, and chewing jaws all froze. Benavides, Thomas, and Teresa shared glances, then the older man spoke. "What did you answer?"

Stone lifted empty palms from the tabletop. "I answered her question, and she reminded me that I've never been through a wormhole before yesterday. She then told me that if I spread any lies or idle speculation, she could block any more of our people from emigrating to Freeland."

"You imply what we already know." Teresa leaned back, creaking her synthwood chair, and crossed her arms. "Deda, I told you."

Benavides' shoulders slumped, and he shook his head as if tired of holding it up for a century. "Why?"

"Deda, you know why," Teresa said, a chill in her mellifluous voice. Thomas grunted in agreement.

Benavides seemed not to hear. "We're three hundred light years from Earth. The UN could send exploration ships three thousand, or thirty thousand, light years further and find empty habitable planets. Why do they push the dregs of Earth onto people like us?"

Why indeed? echoed the Jezhek persona. *There could be a thousand habitable worlds for each UN member—*

I don't make those decisions. I just work here. Stone shoved a forkful of cole slaw into his mouth. His jaw mashed rapidly and vinegar flooded his mouth.

"Jasper knows why, Deda, but is too polite to say it."

Stone writhed his shoulders to abort a shiver.

"We've done the hard work of seeding plants and animals. Building roads and factories and houses. It's easier...."

Teresa opened her mouth to speak. She glanced at Stone and read the set of his facial muscles. She raised her eyebrows and nodded slightly.

"A thousand giant corporations on Earth would love to overcharge on UN contracts for infrastructure on virgin worlds," Stone said. He nodded back at Teresa.

"Jasper has spent decades under the UN's tyranny, Deda." Her voice sounded more gentle. "He knows why. We all know why. Everyone gets to thrill in the abuse of power. Everyone except us. The UN bureaucrats get to order welfare recipients to move hundreds of light years. The power brokers on Earth get to reclaim more civilization from the jungle. The welfare recipients get to maraud across our worlds knowing the UN has their back. All we get is a boot on our neck."

Benavides rotated his beer bottle on the tabletop for a time, then abruptly stopped. He sat taller and the sharp horizontal lines of his face firmed up, like slats of a football player's face mask. "You're right, Teresa. Unless we fight back." He swiveled his head to Stone. "How many of our people want to leave Earth for Freeland?"

"Tens of thousands."

"How many know how to fire a rifle?" Benavides asked.

Stone ran his tongue along the back of his upper teeth. The Jezhek persona fed him impressions. "Tough to say. Maybe a thousand or two served in the US military on UN peacekeeping deployments. About the same number have permits to own hunting rifles."

"That's good–"

"Good, Deda?" Teresa gave her grandfather a gimlet eye. "Two thousand armed men? When the UN will dump, what, two million on us?" She glanced at Stone.

More like ten million. He shrugged, nodded back.

Benavides' face hardened. "Santa Ana's army outnumbered the Texans–"

"Not by a thousand to one." Teresa's words hung in the air.

"And the UN won't let us emigrate with firearms," Stone said.

Benavides raised his beer bottle with a flourish. "Don't worry about that, son." His brown eyes flickered to his right. Outside, LED bulbs cast wan light over his barns and workshops. Benavides drew himself taller. "Two thousand free men can outfight two million slaves. There's nothing more to be said."

"Deda–"

"Nothing more." Benavides' gaze knifed from his granddaughter to his son. "Am I clear?"

Tension bled from the room. "You're clear," Thomas said from Stone's left.

"Of course, Deda. You've spoken." Teresa's voice sounded more melodious than ever.

The corners of Benavides' mouth turned up. "Good. Now we're going to be good hosts and offer Jasper a slice of geneteched pecan pie."

CHAPTER 9

The elevator pinged and the doors slid open. Stone stepped onto the carpeted hallway of the Mezihvezdny's third floor. Stone's gaze passed over the paintings of ranches and robots without seeing them. His report to Gray filled his vision, adding glowing yellow words as he subvoked to his implantable. *...In summary, I suspect Benavides and his family are fabricating rifles at his ranch. I also suspect they received information regarding the Dubai Convention's effects on other colony worlds from UN personnel on Freela–*

A ding sounded in Stone's ear. The middle paragraphs of his report disintegrated. Bright green letters appeared in their place over a translucent gray background.

Call me. Code 390 heading your way.

Stone winced. Not the police code for drunk and disorderly conduct, though about as gratifying. A politician interfering in UNICA affairs.

He jabbed his thumb at his door's lock, then slipped in. Habit smothered his annoyance. A quick sweep of the room for lurkers, then a more thorough scan for eavesdropping devices using electronics concealed in the bottom of his can of shaving gel. Clear. He turned on the lights, drew the blackout panels over the window sheers, opened the safe. From his ankle he unbuckled the holster and laid it in, the 9mm still inside.

He sat on the bed, back against headrest, facing a black video panel on the dresser, mounted on a spindly nanotube-alloy stand. *Call Gray,* he subvoked to his implantable. *Make him look like he's shown on the video panel.*

Gray's shoulders and head appeared. The wall behind his office desk provided a backdrop. The pattern of light and shadow lining Gray's long face and narrow necktie matched the office's artificial lights and agreed with the timestamp in the lower right corner. 8:28 PM EST.

The old man looked testier than usual.

You were about to leave the office when some politician crapped on your desk? Stone asked.

"No. I happened to stay late to catch up on paperwork when word came. I'll end up further behind thanks to this mess."

Someone wants to come to Freeland next week?

A puff of expelled breath flared Gray's nostrils. "They want to go there tomorrow."

They? Gray's words sank deeper. Tomorrow?

"About eight in the morning New York time." Gray turned his head to something out of Stone's view, and the pallid blue light of a video panel washed his face. "–roughly 1045, sunset in Svoboda City." Gray lifted a whisky glass into view, sipped. "Now that we're clear on when, I'll tell you who. First, Chief Minister Yadav of the Ganges Republic, along with his hangers-on and bodyguards."

Stone squinted at the video panel. *Ganges Republic? That's the one with swastikas on its flag?*

Gray blinked. "And I thought you knew nothing about the UN member states on the Indian subcontinent."

I have a cousin who rants every time I see him about the UN allowing the Ganges Republic to fly its flag outside the Secretariat building. No idea why.

"That latter doesn't surprise me." Gray glanced at the off-camera video panel again. "Yadav is facing dissension within his ruling party for appearing soft in his dealings with a religious separatist movement. He announced a few hours ago the UN granted the Ganges Republic eight million resettlement slots on Freeland and he would travel there personally to select locations. He just took to the air and should reach Mach 3 before I hang up."

Stone frowned at a painting of cattle and robots on the wall above and left of the video panel. *The General Assembly can't have approved those resettlement slots yet. What does he hope to achieve by coming here?*

"His grandstanding might persuade the UN to give him those eight million slots. If so, he appears a strong leader to his dissenters and general populace." Gray took another drink of whisky. "More likely, the UN will reject him. Yet if it does, he will claim foreign governments pulled strings in an effort to embarrass his regime and deny the Ganges Republic its place in the sun. Either way, he shores up his domestic support."

Until we topple his regime?

Gray cradled his whisky glass on his palm, his fingers extending up the sides. He swirled the brown liquid. In a hint of furrow in Gray's tall forehead, Stone read a desire to do exactly that. "You know the recognized governments of UN member states are off limits to us. We can only play the hand Yadav and Deshmukh dealt us."

Deshmukh?

"The chief minister of Hindurashtra, a state bordering the Ganges Republic and providing money and materiél to the religious separatist movement I mentioned–"

Hindurashtra? Memories seeped into Stone's mind. *Its government demolished the Taj Mahal a decade back. Because a Muslim king built it, right?*

The whisky glass rose, covering parted lips. "You're a source of surprises today," Gray said.

Stone smirked and made a minimal shake of his head. *I remember that day. Found a UNESCO girl in a bar constantly checking the news feed as the bulldozers rolled in. Tears running down her face....* An easy conquest, and she'd craved emotional connection, or at least the illusion of it.

The smirk dissolved from his facial muscles.

"You've seduced so many women I'm surprised you remember any of them." Gray's hand waved the topic away. "After Yadav's announcement, Deshmukh's government raised a ruckus, as you might expect."

Stone breathed deeply. Thoughts refocused, he asked, *What's the Hindurashtra government's response to Yadav's Freeland visit?* His face fell, intuition answering the question before Gray did.

"Sending its own delegation. Deshmukh and his pack of hangers-on and bodyguards. Your hotel may end up quite crowded."

Shouting matches and even fistfights in the hallways would be the least of Stone's problems. Twelve hours, give or take, until politicians blustered around on a world full of hostiles. Damn. *I can't guarantee their security.*

"Let their bodyguards earn their salaries." Gray glanced at the monitor out of Stone's view. "What security risks did you uncover in your meetings with Kovar and Benavides?"

Kovar's a greedy coward. Benavides, though, is involved in anti-UN activities.

"Tell me."

He's very security-conscious at his ranch. Cams and mikes covering the approaches. He tested my cover with a trick question. The Jezhek persona answered it correctly. Good job by cover stories, I have to give them credit. His granddaughter, Teresa, scraped some skin off my hand, then left for ten minutes. Enough DNA and time to generate my snip profile?

"Yes."

Clearly they had reason to suspect a stranger from Earth as being a UN operative. They were involved in Dragon's death. Stone shrugged. *I'm here talking to you, so clearly my snip profile matched my cover story. Have to give credit to the genomics tech too. When Teresa returned after running my snip profile, she and Benavides opened up to me. They strongly hinted they have inside information on how the Dubai Convention transforms colony worlds.*

"The evidence weighs more and more that a UN employee is giving them intelligence."

They also implied they fabricate rifles at their ranch. Stone blew out a breath. For all Gray's secret power, dead heads of UN member governments would weaken him. *Yadav and Deshmukh's bodyguards won't be able to stop a sniper. Especially when the spy inside the UN offices here gives the sniper Yadav and Deshmukh's itineraries and photographs. Do I need to change my mission?*

Gray swirled his whisky and studied it for a time. "You have proof Benavides is building rifles on his ranch?"

No.

"Acquire some. Photographs would help, and recorded admissions and physical samples would help even more. Relay any evidence you find to me and I'll instruct Director Kroebel to lean on Chief Executive Schmied to arrest Benavides and his family."

Stone cocked his head. *Local police didn't arrest Benavides for the vandalism against Kovar or Schmied. The police have taken Benavides' side. I wouldn't trust them.*

"I don't. After you acquire the evidence, I'll have the director give Schmied and the police commissioner an ultimatum. Arrest Benavides themselves or UN peacekeepers will come through the wormhole and do it."

Provided I get you enough evidence. Twelve hours to find it. The corners of Stone's mouth lifted. *Action in pursuit of a clear goal. Nothing better.*

"If you cannot acquire it in time, your fallback assignment is to foil any attempt by Benavides to assassinate Yadav or Deshmukh."

Understood.

"Anything happen today that your truck's transponder didn't alert me to?"

I've laid enough groundwork with a hotel employee to probably get into the hotel's computers and find security footage of exactly who returned Dragon to his room.

"That's a low priority."

Agreed. The last thing, a keyhole kop questioned me as Jezhek. I played it with mild hostility and she let me go with a warning.

"Yadav and Deshmukh's impending visit should keep her busy. But do stay below her radar." Gray lifted his whisky glass. "Anything else? Gray out." The older man's image vanished.

Silence filled the hotel room for a moment. Then Stone laughed deeply. The sound echoed off beige wallpaper and the cheap painting above the video panel, likely punched through the flimsy wallboard to raise eyebrows in the next room. Stone did not care. The day just ended of method acting the role of Jasper Jezhek, gathering information through quiet conversation, gave way to what really mattered. Action. The ultimate extreme sport, triumph or death.

Stone would love his work even if the UN's destiny didn't turn on it.

How to infiltrate Benavides' weapons workshop? Heart thudding, Stone grinned. He'd find a way. Not a gillie suit–he'd left his at UNICA headquarters, and the array of cameras and microphones ringing Benavides' house and buildings would pick up enough output from even the most concealing suit to betray him.

His grin widened, pushed his head back. He had better camouflage than any gillie suit Dragon might have used. Stone laughed. *Isn't that right, Jasper?*

In the depths of his mind, the Jezhek persona remained quiet.

Fingers rap-rapped on the door to the room. Stone's head whipped up. He slid off the bed and with deft fingers opened the safe. The .357 seemed to leap into his hand. Pistol muffled against his body, he racked the slide. He held the pistol muzzle up, so close to his nose to catch the faint smells of oil and plastic. The energy spiraling in him since Gray ended the call coiled tighter, faster.

In the hallway, the person rap-rapped again. Stone padded two steps and checked the door's peephole.

The blue eyes of Teresa Benavides stared back. Her plush lips remained closed, corners curled up, a coy smile. She wore a thin, pale blue jacket, zipped to the top and collar turned up, covering the sides of her neck. From her face, he knew exactly why she'd come.

Gray tasked him to surveill the Benavides family. Up close and personal....

Stone opened the door with his free hand. The security bar stopped the door after two inches. A smirk formed, visible to her from the left side of his face. "I didn't order room service."

Teresa's coy smile remained. Her fingers tugged the jacket's zipper halfway down. Cleavage of creamy skin, a waft of perfume dabbed there.

"Special delivery," she said.

"Need to get my pen to sign for it." Stone shut the door, then laid his pistol back in the safe. A moment later he swung the security bar against the wall. He turned the handle and pulled the door fully open. "Set it over–"

Teresa pressed her hands against his chest and pushed him toward the bed. Her lips parted now, mashing his mouth. His legs backed into the bed. Stone grabbed her waist and lifted her as he tumbled backward.

The door's automatic closer clicked shut. Teresa straddled him, her hair spilling into his face, trapping the warmth of their heavy breaths. She kept kissing him and pulled her jacket zipper the rest of the way down. She wore nothing underneath.

Stone grinned. "–on the bed." He closed his hands on her flanks and flung her onto her back. He pressed his body on hers. Fingers yanked at belts and buttons. Her jacket flew to the floor, landed with a clunk. The rest of their clothes followed. His hands traced her smooth warm skin, her soft curves, her slick–

She moaned. "Now."

The Genomics tech's words nudged at Stone. He slid over Teresa and pulled out the nightstand drawer. He ripped a wrapped condom off the strip, then tore the wrapper.

With her elbows, she pushed herself a few inches toward the headboard. "What kind of girl do you take me for?"

The corners of Stone's mouth edged up. "The kind who comes to strange men's hotel rooms."

"Only if those strange men are from Earth." She rolled her eyes. "I want babies, but not nine months from now. I'm on the pill."

"Good for you." Stone put on the condom.

Teresa slid an inch back down the bed. Her shoulders eased into the pillow, and the coy smile drifted back to her face. "No prophylactic next time."

"Sure. But right now, it's this time."

Afterward, breaths caught and hearts slowed. Teresa stared at the ceiling through lidded eyes, a half-smile glazing her features. She simulated that self-deluding zone where they imagined a roll in the hay might lead to lifelong love.

Not a bad act by an amateur.

Stone slipped off the filled condom and knotted the end. He dropped the sticky latex on the bed next to him.

Teresa propped herself on one elbow, blond hair loose over her eye. She ran her free hand along Stone's chest. His curled hairs slid off the buffed ends of her fingernails.

"You didn't scratch me with those."

Mirth touched the corners of her mouth and her one exposed eye. "Did you deserve getting scratched?"

"I got exactly what I deserved," Stone said. He smirked again. "So did you."

She exhaled. The mirth leaked out with her breath. "I need to clean up." Her smooth arm brushed the hairs on his abdomen, reaching over him toward the condom. "I'll flush that fool thing for you."

He twisted onto his side, facing her. His hand lifted in the direction of the desk near the window. "The trashcan's good enough."

She slowly drew in a breath, then her coy smile returned. "I'm sure it is." She rolled off the bed, crouched on firm legs to pick up her jacket and other clothes. Moments later she went to the bathroom. The latchbolt snicked shut. The rustle of water from the shower sounded under the closed door.

Stone's smirk vanished. He slid off the bed and dropped the condom in the trashcan under the desk. With deft motions he dressed.

He approached the closet. Light slipping under the bathroom door leached color from his trousers and polo shirts. Quickly, quietly, he pulled on clothes, stepped into shoes. The shower changed notes for a moment, the sound of Teresa adjusting the angle. Good. She thought she had him fooled. Teresa could have only one reason for being so opposed to a condom earlier and so eager to dispose it for him now. The UN employee working with Benavides gave her reason to doubt the snip profile of Jezhek.

Stone reached for the room safe. The UN employee knew Gray's agent would be revealed by a snip mismatch between his skin sample and his unmodified genomic data.

His hand froze, a sudden chill standing up the hairs on his arms.

The UN employee worked for Gray.

Heat flooded Stone's chest. Someone in UNICA's local office spied for Benavides. He had to tell Gray. But first, deal with Teresa. He extended his hand toward the safe–

Light bloomed behind him. The bathroom door bonged against its stop. Stone swung his head. The bathroom lights silhouetted Teresa with a pistol. An angular, black alloy .38 aimed at his chest.

"Don't move," she said, her voice like tinkling icicles. "Whoever the hell you are."

CHAPTER 10

Stone eyed her .38, then put on a cockeyed grin. "If that's your kink, you should have told me before, not after." *Message to Gray,* he subvoked to his wearable. *Codes 24 and 32, on my poz.*

The shower ran unheeded behind her. Teresa inclined her head toward the door. She held the .38 steady. "We're going down the fire stairs and into the side parking lot. You'll be quiet or I'll shoot. Clear?"

"What are you going on about?" He raised his pitch. "We're on the same side and you're kidnapping me?"

Codes 24 and 32, now. Teresa Benavides pierced cover story.

His wearable superimposed sickly yellow text over her midriff. *Wireless networking not available.*

Her gaze flicked from his neck to his face. "Don't bother calling your masters." She twisted her hips slightly, drawing his eye to the print of a small flat box against her jacket's front pocket. "I'm jamming your signals."

Stone's tongue wanted to lick his lips. He stopped it. Inhaled. Jamming his calls also meant his biotelemetry would no longer reach UNICA headquarters. Gray would respond.

Just like he responded for Dragon.

A fist thumped the door. Teresa stepped laterally that way, her gaze locked on Stone. Her free hand groped air, found the door handle.

Her uncle, Thomas, loomed in the doorway. Two men about Teresa's age, taller and broader-shouldered than her uncle, stout as offensive linemen, stood behind him.

"Boys," Thomas said, and an extended family resemblance leaped out at Stone. "Grab his arms."

Thomas stepped back and the young men passed around him. The one on the left stood only six-two. Stone labeled him Guard. His half-brother or cousin on the right–Tackle–had an extra two inches and fifteen pounds. Neutralize both, grab Teresa's pistol, force his way past Thomas... Long odds.

Guard and Tackle raised hands thick enough to wrestle steers or punch cows. They gripped Stone's lean but firm upper arms and yanked him out the door.

Thomas led the way toward the fire stairs. Trapped between Guard and Tackle, Stone followed, six feet behind. Too far to kick Thomas in the ribs. They allowed him to walk. Not out of respect, just to save the energy otherwise required to drag him. Behind Stone, Teresa's boots clomped along the carpet, close enough that the mingled scents of her perfume and the .38's black alloy reached him.

The automatic closer slammed shut his room door, a sound echoing down the empty hallway. A tense silence held sway, as if the Connors and Melissas cowered in their beds and pretended not to know what happened outside their rooms.

Stone glanced up at a hemispherical camera mount on the ceiling. Video of the Benavides family abducting him... would be deleted from the hotel's security server, just as surely as the video of the Benavides family carrying Dragon to his room to be murdered had been deleted.

Seducing Natalie to access the security server would have availed Stone nothing. At least she wouldn't have held him at gunpoint afterward.

Down the fire stairs and out the side entrance. The river rustled to the right, lights from buildings on the far bank dappled by oak foliage. Under LED lamps, cars and trucks waited passively in the parking lot. Another vehicle waited, parked along the curb near the hotel. A hefty pickup truck befitting Guard and Tackle, flared fenders over four wheels on the rear axle, hitched to a twenty-foot, windowless trailer of shiny aluminum.

The truck's engine hummed up and the trailer lowered its rear door. "Inside," Thomas said to Guard and Tackle, then went to the truck's driver-side door.

Aluminum shrieked when the rear door touched asphalt, becoming a ramp. The shadows inside the trailer remained strong, denying Stone details of what lay within. Traces of cleaning fluid, no stinks of straw or manure, at least. The two beefy men tromped up the ramp into the interior. Stone didn't resist.

Behind him, the aluminum ramp rang with Teresa's footsteps. "Close," she said, echoes betraying her location as just inside the trailer, near its left side.

An electric motor hummed. Stone's mouth went dry. This might be his last best chance to escape–

He flexed his right biceps. Tackle tightened his grip even further. Forget escape.

The ramp lifted, deepening the shadows inside the trailer. An embryonic smile nudged the corners of Stone's mouth. *Gray wants you to surveill them, after all.*

The last sliver of lamplight night narrowed and disappeared. "Lights," Teresa said.

At the top of each sidewall, three evenly-spaced LEDs filled the trailer with sharp white light. The aluminum walls gleamed and black anti-slip panels lined the floor. Four jump seats clustered near the front, two on the front wall and one on each sidewall.

A steel bar mounted on the front wall held two pairs of handcuffs dangling toward the jump seat on the right. The corner seam held a ring, also made of steel, near the floor. A pair of ankle cuffs lay on the floor, secured to the ring by a chain as jumbled as a sleeping snake.

"Cuff him so we can go," Teresa said.

Guard and Tackle dragged him between them. When they reached the jumpseat, they wheeled around to face the trailer's rear door. Teresa stood near the center of the space, next to a floor-to-ceiling steel cabinet on her left, and trained the .38 on Stone's chest. The black alloy seemed to suck in the trailer's light.

"Sit," Teresa said. Guard lifted his boot and pushed down the seat. Both beefy men pushed Stone's arms toward his shoulders.

He bent his knees. His rump landed on rough fabric and a thin cushion. They straightened his arms toward the bar above the backrest. Tackle handcuffed Stone first, Guard next. The steel's cold banded his wrists. Stone watched every motion. Amateurs. He knew half a second in advance each time they weakened their grip on his arms or distracted themselves with the handcuffs. Good to know when he had an opportunity to escape.

Assuming he needed to escape.

The .38's muzzle stared at him like an unblinking eye. "Feet on the floor."

"I'll cause no trouble." He kept his soles flat on the anti-slip pad. Guard untangled the chain and clapped on the ankle cuffs.

"Good," Teresa said. "Time to go." Tiny muscles flexed in her neck. Guard and Tackle took the two jumpseats flanking Stone and each strapped in. Their hot breath and sweat crowded Stone's corner of the trailer. With the .38 in her right hand, Teresa held onto a cabinet handle. She bent her knees, dropping her center of gravity, and a moment later the trailer pulled forward.

Stone mapped the acceleration, slowing, and turns of the trailer onto his sense of the parking lot and the street. A right turn onto Novy Morava Avenue. Heading for the bridge, then, and ultimately the Benavides ranch.

Thirty minutes of drive time. Enough? It would have to be.

Teresa thumbed the safety and slipped her .38 into the right front pocket of her jacket. She pivoted to the cabinet and turned a handle with her right hand. She reached inside. The steel door hid the objects she sought. He didn't need to see. She'd pull out a lancet and–

She closed and secured the cabinet door with her left. Stone's gaze locked on her right. He nodded. She held a pen-sized plastic object, a pushbutton on one end and a recess in the other. A lancet, push the button and a tiny pin would jab out of the recess with enough force to draw blood. Trapped between her hand and the lancet, a transparent tube as narrow as rice vermicelli from that Vietnamese restaurant on 71st flopped against her index finger.

"Don't bother," Stone said. "Drawing blood to run my snip profile. It will confirm what your contact already told you."

"Oh?" The trailer turned. With her left hand on the cabinet's door handle, Teresa pulled her body into the curve.

A left turn onto Blaha Boulevard? Not over the bridge. Not the shortest path to Benavides' ranch. Stone blinked. Did another bridge span the Novy Morava away from Svoboda City?

Or did she plan to dump his body far from her grandfather's weapons workshops to deflect UN attention?

"My name is not Jasper Jezhek. The snip profile you ran from the cells you scraped off my palm was engineered through a skin-penetrating DNA vector. The DNA from my blood cells will give you my true snip profile, which isn't Czech."

The trailer's course straightened and the towing truck accelerated. "I don't care who you aren't."

"My name is Simon St. Clair. I'm with the UN Interstellar Transport Bureau. ITB sent me here to alert you before it's too late."

The truck slowed down. Teresa leaned back and it came to a stop. A traffic light, probably. She strode forward and shoved the lancet against the tip of his right index finger. A snick and pain pricked his fingertip. She pocketed the lancet, then squeezed a deep red drop out of his finger. The blood drop glistened in the LED lights, until she touched the floppy transparent tube to it. Blood capillaried up the tube.

She returned to the cabinet, did something he couldn't see. She shut the cabinet door and sat on the nearest jumpseat before the presumed traffic light turned green. Inside the cabinet, electronics hummed and whirred.

Teresa strapped herself in. She gave a tight-lipped smile, as pleasing and cold as her voice. "You're quite good at improvised lies, Mr.–" Her tone provided the air-quotes, "'St. Clair.'"

Only half-improvised–he'd picked the name from storefronts in a small town in southeast England. "Allow me to prove my bona fides. I have intelligence for you. The morning of the day after tomorrow, two heads of government from UN member states will come through the wormhole."

Her eyebrow jumped up. "Names?"

"Yadav, from the Ganges Republic, and Deshmukh, from Hindurasthra."

"Morning? Do you have a more precise time?"

"0500," he said. His elevated arms made his shoulders ache. Too early to ask her to remove the cuffs.

Teresa leaned back against her jumpseat's rough fabric. Though partially shadowed, the subvocal patch electrodes on her neck looked immobile. Her eyes peered at him, like a marksman through a firing slit. "Too late for what, Mr. St. Clair?"

"From assassinating Yadav, Deshmukh, or both."

A tight-lipped smile flexed Teresa's cheeks. "What kind of girl do you take me for?"

He met her gaze. "The kind who would do anything to preserve her people from becoming outnumbered two-hundred-to-one on their home planet."

"Seems if I were that kind of girl, I'd want to kill them."

"Do that and they become martyrs. The UN will allow their successors to send twenty million settlers, not ten, and we won't be able to stop them–"

"We?"

He rattled the handcuff chains. "I represent a faction inside ITB that's trying to soften the blow the Dubai Convention inflicts on colony worlds. We're working behind the scenes for a low settler count to Freeland, with most settlers from Europe or North America."

She sniffed out a breath. "Why would your ITB faction care what we want?" The truck stopped at another traffic light.

"We don't. Fewer settlers on existing colonies means more demand for new colonies. That means more exploration ships, more settler transport ships, and more wormholes to build and tow."

The truck pulled forward. "You just want to expand your bureaucracy."

"Everyone does. But we can expand ours while benefiting you."

The truck accelerated to a higher speed. Smooth asphalt hissed under the tires.

She took him west of Svoboda City, toward the wormhole. Surely not to the wormhole itself. Unless she planned to dump his corpse at the ITB checkpoint. A bolder statement than breaking windows–

A ding sounded inside the cabinet. Teresa pulled a small tablet computer from her jeans pocket. "Snip profile has your ancestry as predominantly Anglo-Saxon, with traces of Dutch, Jewish, Spanish, and–African?"

Stone shrugged. "You know those English sailors. At sea for months, any port in a storm, right?"

She subvoked. Her gaze traced lines of text on the tablet screen. "The names Simon and St. Clair fit with Anglo-Saxon ancestry."

A flick of her wrist, and the tablet's magnetic lid snapped shut. "You've told me who you claim to be. Your story might even be true. Now tell me about someone else." She leaned forward against the jumpseat straps. "Who is my contact?"

The next few seconds could sign his death warrant. His story would work if the UN turncoat worked for the keyhole kops. Or UNICA. It would even work if an amateur watched enough movies about tradecraft to only communicate electronically. But if not.... then his lies bought at least a few minutes of life. "His name is Mustafa Akbar."

Her cheeks flexed again in another tight-lipped smile. Her hand drifted toward her jacket's front right pocket. "No it isn't."

"Of course he gave you a different name. Standard opsec. That's operational–"

"Security. I figured that out."

An amateur, but sharp. A shame she resisted the UN, rather than accept its supremacy.

"Akbar, you said?" Teresa shook her head. "He doesn't look Arab."

"You can't tell. Software masks in televisual communication provide real-time false faces, false voices, even false accents and dictions. Besides, he's Indian."

She squinted. Not at Stone, but through him. At memories of the UN turncoat through the filter of his lies. "Indian."

Stone's abdominal muscles unclenched. She'd never met the turncoat in person. "He's part of the Muslim minority from the Ganges Republic. A cabal of Muslims plots a coup attempt. The plotters put together inside information that both Yadav and Deshmukh would travel here and persuaded Akbar to assist them by recruiting a patsy–" He winced and turned his gaze from her. "–to assassinate them."

Rather good for an improvised lie. His gaze drifted up to her face. Her blue eyes squinted in thought.

The truck slowed. The ITB checkpoint already? Then the trailer turned to the right. The truck sped up a little. Throughout the trailer, aluminum squeaked from potholes and bumps in the road.

Not to the ITB checkpoint. Where did she take him?

Teresa suddenly spoke. "Your story would explain why Akbar might want Yadav killed. But not Deshmukh. He's the president of another country, you said? Akbar would want him alive to frame with Yadav's assassination."

"Ganges Republic Muslims hate Hindurasthra. Deshmukh's government destroyed the Taj Mahal and other Muslim cultural sites a decade ago. It's a double win for Akbar if he gets you to assassinate them both."

The truck slowed again. Another turn, to the left, and now the truck rolled slowly over a washboard of a gravel road. The trailer rattled, almost smothering the crunch of pebbles under the tires.

The last leg of the journey. To where?

Stone's shoulders and upper arms burned. "Now that I've told you everything, you can take off the cuffs."

Her tight-lipped smile returned. "Leave a girl one kink, Mr. 'St. Clair.'"

CHAPTER 11

The trailer bounced along the gravel road, rattling Stone against the jumpseat's thin cushion. The squeal of the trailer's metal surfaces rubbing together and the rattle of the washboarded road grated in Stone's ears. Teresa remained silent, her gaze on her tablet screen. Did she subvoke to the UN turncoat, checking Stone's story? He couldn't tell. Guard and Tackle hunkered down behind beefy arms folded across their chests.

Thirty breaths later, the truck slowed for a right turn. The two men sat further upright and shared glances with one another and Teresa. The trailer thumped over metal rods. A cattle guard, the Jezhek persona had called it at the entrance to Benavides' ranch.

Whatever his destination, Stone neared it.

He lolled his head, listening for ambient sounds. The truck followed a lane of gravel and packed dirt. A faint echo suggested they drove past a building, perhaps a house or barn. The echo faded.

Stone licked dry lips. Teresa might take him straight to an empty ditch about six feet long.

They continued along the lane for a dozen breaths. The truck slowed, turned hard to the right, then backed up.

The trailer rolled onto a firm, quiet surface. The hum of the truck's motor reflected off hard surfaces all around the trailer. Stone drooped his head, scraping as much data from the soundscape reaching his ears as he could. Inside a workshop or barn–with a double height interior, if he heard right–on a concrete floor.

He let out a breath. Strong though they might be, Guard and Tackle couldn't dig a shallow grave in a concrete slab.

A chill ran across his aching shoulders. Concrete was an easy surface to hose down blood.

The truck slowed. One last shudder swayed Stone's suspended arms.

Teresa unbuckled and stood. She pulled her .38 from her pocket and released the safety. "Cuff his hands together, behind him. Then disconnect his ankle cuffs from the wall."

Stone's peripheral vision fell away. Energy raced through his body, like an electric current seeking a ground. A second with both hands free could be enough–

The trailer's rear door remained closed. Even if he, unarmed, could overwhelm the two linemen and wrest the .38 from Teresa, Thomas Benavides, undoubtedly watching through hidden cameras, would leave Stone locked inside.

One by one, Guard and Tackle opened the cuffs holding up his arms. Stone's hands tingled with recirculating blood. "Where are we?" he asked.

"That's not important," Teresa said. The two men yanked Stone out of the jumpseat by his forearms. They pulled his hands behind his back.

"You're putting me on ice while you try to verify my story," Stone said. "I understand why you want to, but if you tip off Akbar, things will go much worse for Freeland in the long run."

Teresa's voice turned as bleak and disinterested as a winter wind down concrete canyons. "Or he'll demolish your lies." Guard and Tackle snapped the handcuffs around Stone's wrists. Tackle kneeled and released the ankle cuffs from their wall-mounting ring.

"Go to the door. Slowly." Teresa gestured with her .38.

Stone took one waddling penguin step. He looked down at the

short chain between his ankles, then up at her. "Quickly isn't an option."

"Leave the smart-ass comments to the person with the gun. Move."

He shuffled across the trailer's no-slip padding toward the rear door. Guard and Tackle followed him, a ragged note to their breaths. They might guide a bull the same way.

"Open," Teresa said. An electric motor hummed. The rear door gapped away from the trailer's ceiling. Antiseptic light entered. Concrete block walls. Corrugated metal ceiling. Whiffs of dried grass, dirt, hay, and cattle.

Stone stopped six inches from the rear door. The ramp scraped to a halt on the concrete slab. Eight feet beyond the ramp's edge, the slab ended at an animal pen of pitted dirt. A gate of green tubular steel, four feet high and eight wide, formed the pen's near side. Concrete block walls on the pen's left and right. A trough at waist height ran the length of the right-hand wall, ending at the pen's far side, where another green steel gate separated the pen from a field empty under a deep black sky.

His eyes briefly widened. From the northeastern–the back left–corner of the pen, a radio transmission from his implantable might have line-of-sight to Svoboda City, free of interference from concrete and metal. Provided Teresa left the barn to contact the UN turncoat, and took her jammer with her.

"Get him in," Teresa said.

Tackle grunted at the other. Guard went wide around Stone. The ramp clattered with his footsteps. He unlatched the green gate and swung it toward the truck. The gate's bottom corner scraped along a pale, arcuate gouge in the concrete.

A push on Stone's right shoulder forced him to writhe, but he kept his balance. "You heard her," Tackle said.

Stone shuffled down the ramp, two inches per step. His soles thudded on the concrete slab. He stepped from concrete onto the pen's floor. Deep holes about six to eight inches wide, their bottoms sunk in shade, pitted the dry, packed dirt. *Cattle hoofprints made when rain and cow piss soaked the ground.* Stone wobbled and carefully picked his way forward.

Behind him, the gate's corner groaned along the gouge in the slab. Hinges creaked. The gate's latch rattled closed.

He peered over the tubular steel at the back of the pen, into the deep night. In the tufted grass, insects buzzed like cars humming along the FDR. He tuned them out to listen to the gate latch behind him. Nothing. Just a slip latch. Flex one piece of metal and kick out, and the gate would crash into anyone standing nearby.

Hell, the gate itself only came up to his chest. Grab the gate's top rail and jump over–

The gate keeps cattle in. Right now, you have the same number of hands they do.

Stone scowled into the night. The insect buzz made him long for the city. A new suite of sounds joined the insects, from somewhere out of sight to his left. Keening machine tools and curt male voices.

"Keep an eye on him," Teresa said to the two men. "Take these."

Stone turned slowly. Tackle held the .38, muzzle down. His thick left hand engulfed a gray plastic box, covering a glowing green status light on the box's edge.

She might be an amateur, but not amateur enough.

Teresa went around the trailer to the truck's passenger door. Stone glimpsed Thomas Benavides through the driver's side mirror. Hidden by the trailer, the passenger door thumped shut. A rubber squeak of turning tires and the truck pulled forward, toward a rolled-up door on the far side of the barn. The truck towed the trailer into the dark night, then turned right, in the direction of the machine tools and male voices.

The trailer's taillights glowed like demon eyes before leaving Stone's sight. How long would it take her to sound out the turncoat and conclude he'd lied?

Less than twenty minutes and they'd kill him.

Guard puffed out his chest. "What are you looking at?"

"I don't know." Stone pulled his gaze from the rolled-up doorway and the faint sounds of tools and working men. "You tell me."

Tackle slid his empty left hand from his jeans' front pocket, then thumped his hand onto Guard's shoulder. "One of us is going to watch him from each side."

"Good idea."

"I know."

Stone eyed the distance between where Tackle stood near the gouge in the concrete slab and the northeastern corner of the pen. Twenty-five or thirty feet. Far enough for Stone to get out of range from Tackle's jammer? Not enough information to guess. But if Tackle watched Stone from the empty field, Stone's communication would go through the jammer's active field.

One centering breath. "Seems like you ought to come outside, big guy," Stone said.

Tackle squared his broad shoulders to Stone. "We didn't ask you."

"You didn't. What about him? Just because you're bigger and Teresa thinks you're more reliable doesn't mean he has to trudge all the way around the barn."

Guard frowned. "This Sinclair guy's got a point."

"He's playing us, *čurák*. Maybe he thinks you're pretty and wants to look at you in better light."

"Wha–?"

"Take a shortcut through the pen next to his. I got to be the one watching him the whole time. Got it?" Tackle rotated his right arm at the shoulder. The .38 in his hand twisted in the bright white light. With his left hand, Tackle shoved Guard's forearm. "Get moving."

Bulky torso hunched, Guard trudged forward and slipped out of sight behind one of the pen's concrete block walls. Hinges whined at the neighboring pen's gate.

Stone shuffled his feet to turn his body. After the harsh light inside the barn, the moonless night soothed his eyes. He took a tiny step toward the pen's corner–

"Not you," Tackle said. "You stay put until he gets out there."

Stone looked over his shoulder and raised his eyebrows. He wiggled his fingers behind his back. "Come on. I just want some fresh air."

The open doorway at the far end of the barn framed Tackle's bulk. He shifted his weight from side to side, and the bright overheads lit up twitchy eyes. "Stay put till he gets in position." He jerked his head an eighth of a turn, then lifted the .38 across his chest as if he'd just remembered it.

Stone shrugged. The UN turncoat must have warned them about UNICA's close combat training. He twisted at the waist to show more of his upper body to Tackle. "Will do."

Guard's boots clomped across the hard, jagged ground of the neighboring pen. Another gate latch rattled, more hinges squeaked. Guard came into view, his feet bending over tufts of sprangletop and crushing chips of dry, odorless cow manure. He stopped in the field twenty feet from the back gate of Stone's pen, his feet just inside a soft-edged rectangle of diffuse barn light, his head a gray rock against the moonless night sky.

"Now?" Stone asked.

Tackle grunted and nodded. Stone shuffled toward the corner of the pen. The ground close to the sidewall flattened out enough for him to step without fear of falling.

Out of sight, from the direction Teresa and her uncle had traveled, came a clang of metal on metal.

He rested his left shoulder against the concrete block wall, and leaned his chest against the tubular steel gate. The slip latch rattled.

Guard stiffened. "What the hell are you doing?"

Stone looked at the southeastern horizon. The sky, washed out by Svoboda City's light pollution, backlit a stand of tall locust trees at the far side of the field. Leaves rustled in a breeze that cooled Stone's face. A chill crept over his bare forearms. "Getting some air."

A grunt. Guard's shoulders relaxed.

No need to look in the direction of Svoboda City for Stone's implantable to transmit. Stone's gaze drifted across the dark field. The faint hiss of a carrier tone calmed him. He'd gotten out of range of the jammer in Tackle's pocket.

First he tried a message to Gray. A receiver in the UN quarter might pick up and relay it through the wormhole. *Codes 24 and 32.* Operative captured, operative in danger. *Location is a ranch west-northwest of Svoboda City, near the wormhole.*

No answer. No surprise. Many links comprised the comm chain

between him and Gray. A rescue mission would take hours to reach him.

Time to rescue himself.

Through his implantable, Stone subvoked to his truck. *Come to this position, maximum permissible speed.*

The carrier hiss half-filled Stone's ears. He clamped his lips together. Hadn't the truck heard?

Coming, it replied. *Estimated arrival in 18:04.* Stone's implantable overlaid two indicators in his vision: a countdown clock in the lower right that panned with the movements of his head and a filled green outline of the truck ghosting inside the stand of locusts.

18:01, 18:00, 17:59... If the truck didn't arrive until after the UN turncoat convinced Teresa that Stone lied...

He leaned against the gate, head up. Unfamiliar constellations crept across the night sky. Behind him, Tackle's boots from time to time scraped the concrete slab. A shift in the winds carried a breeze through the barn to Stone's bare forearms. He sniffed a faint, oily scent. Machine tools roared and thumped in the distance.

What were Teresa and her family building? And why here rather than the Benavides' ranch?

For that matter, where was *here*?

The truck's green ghost crept along. Seconds ticked by. The truck might drive more slowly than its prediction; each second could be fractionally longer than a real second.

Stone leaned against the concrete block wall, face calm, while the breeze turned drops of sweat into frigid pinpricks on the back of his neck. Fifteen minutes. Ten. Five.

Maybe he'd lied so well Teresa believed him? He let his eyes close, then waggled his head side to side. Leave wishing to fools.

His wearable now superimposed the green ghost truck on the concrete block walling the pen's far side. Two minutes till the truck expected to arrive. The green ghost drifted to the right, toward the barn's interior. Toward the jammer in Tackle's pocket.

Interference blurred the green ghost's edges. The truck drove on. Stone traced back the turns and guesstimated speeds of his travel. Still on the main highway? Or had it turned toward the last dirt road before the cattle guard? Static from the jammer diced the ghost truck, then obliterated it.

From the middle distance, to the right of the barn's open door, steel clanged against more steel. Perhaps a door flung open. Teresa might head his way this very moment–

Stone drew in a breath. The inhalation steadied him, but incompletely. Where was the truck? On the dirt He swallowed dryly. He would need to shout instructions to the truck for his plan to succeed.

Motion behind Tackle, outside the rolled-up gate, made Stone whip his head around.

Teresa's cowboy boots thumped on the concrete slab. Her mouth showed a grim line, and her eyes drilled into Stone with clamped anger.

Behind her, fifty yards away and around a turn in the gravel lane, bobbed the headlights of his truck.

CHAPTER 12

Her voice rang clear and cold through the barn. "His story didn't check." She nodded at Tackle, once, a silent sentence of death.

Tackle nodded back at her. The truck rounded the turn and faced the rolled-up door head-on. The man squinted into the headlights. "Who's that?"

The truck's tires crunched gravel into the lane. With two human shapes in its radars and infrared imagers, the truck crept along. *Come on. You might not hear me shout in time.* Stone backed up against the concrete block wall, his feet on untrampled dirt.

Teresa stopped and looked over her shoulder. The truck's headlights silhouetted her tall, strong figure. She extended her hand behind her and to the side, toward Tackle. "His friends."

The truck rolled forward. The faint hum of the electric motor reached Stone like the buzz of a distant insect.

Teresa raised her voice. "Kill him now."

"But," Tackle said, "What about–"

She whirled, hair whipping like a carnival ride. "Now!"

"Cornerback!" Stone shouted at the truck. "Full speed! At me!"

The truck's tires flung gravel. The electric motor thrummed. A hiss from the front shocks, headlight beams jolting up and down on the wall opposite Stone. Front tires on the barn's concrete slab. Another jolt of the headlights, a hiss of four tires on concrete.

"No!" shouted Tackle. A scream, hot and harsh and utterly unlike her voice, came from Teresa. Metal collided with something meaty.

"Gate head on!" Stone shouted. His heart pounded once, a fraction of a second that seemed to last an eternity. "Brake!" He shut his eyes and turned his head away.

Tires screeched. Metal crumpled and bolts tore free, harsh sounds amplified by the concrete block walls of the holding pen.

The truck slumped, front tires on the hoof-pocked ground. The mangled gate leaned against the radiator grill and the buckled trough angled up the far wall. Only the left headlight glowed. The truck's right headlight gaped blindly, a dark hole with jagged plastic edges.

Stone waddled toward the truck's cab. "Open the door!"

The driver's door popped open. Six inches at the most. Dammit. Stone flexed his fingers uselessly behind his back. "Further!"

"I've opened the door as far as I can," the truck said through his implantable and transcranial stim, in its bland brunette voice.

He waddled faster against the chain linking his lower legs. Step, step, st– His right ankle almost rolled outward on an uneven patch of ground. Somehow he kept his balance. Get in the truck, now.

"Hey!" shouted Guard from the field. Light from the barn's interior still falling short of his face. Good. "Hey! What are you doing?"

Stone reached the driver's door. He wedged his left elbow between the door and the post and twisted at the waist. The door swung further open, leaving a two-foot gap.

"Hey!" Guard's voice came closer. "Stop!"

Stone bent his knees and jumped into the cab. His left arm slammed onto the cushioned driver's seat. His knees slammed the hard metal of the door post. Pain shot up his legs. He pulled them closer to his body. "Close the door!"

"I can't," the truck replied

He twisted his body half-upright. Both feet touched the floor under the steering wheel. Damn, his knees hurt. "I'm clear, close it!"

"I lack the ability to close the door."

Stone twisted more. He sat almost normally in the driver's seat, except for his cuffed hands behind his back. The headlight lit up Guard's stern arm reaching over the pen's rear gate for the latch.

"Reverse, full speed!"

The rear tires shrieked. The truck drove backward, jostling Stone with every bump in the pitted ground under the front tires. For a moment, the front tires caught on the edge of the concrete slab. One more jostle and the front tires hopped up and onto the slab.

Faster. The stink of peeled-out rubber. Blurred steel walls and a loft of vomit-green hay through the half-open driver's door. In the rear view mirror, a beefy male figure on one bent knee, his other lower leg mangled. A .38 in his hand. Stone ducked. A gunshot roared inside the barn–

The open driver's door slammed into Tackle. It hung loosely on its hinges and Tackle slid down to the concrete. His mangled body, blood pooling on the slab near the dropped handgun, receded from Stone. Teresa stepped forward. Her eyes regarded her kinsman. Despite the growing distance, the whites of her eyes blazed with anguish.

Stone's truck raced off the concrete, onto gravel.

Teresa turned her head, eyes narrow as lenses focusing a white-hot laser right between Stone's eyes. She squatted and kept her gaze on him. Her hand groped for the .38 through the seeping viscous crimson of Tackle's blood.

"Slew us around!" Stone said to the truck. "Then full speed to the wormhole!"

The truck turned sharply, centrifugal force shoving Stone toward the open, dangling door. He clenched his legs and jammed his back against the seat. Gravel sprayed, then the rear wheels felt loose. Grass under the tires. A glance inside the barn showed Teresa rising, the angular black .38 in hands smeared with blood.

Stone leaned toward the center of the cab. The truck shifted into forward gear and accelerated into a right-hand turn, pulling the right side of Stone's body down.

A distant gunshot. A rain of glass shards tinkled onto the rear seat. Air whistled through a hole in the windshield. Another shot, another, one more. A second bullet through the rear window, exiting the windshield.

"Faster!" he called at the truck. Acceleration pressed him against the backrest. Wind howled through the holes in the windshield as the truck followed the curving lane.

No more shots. He stole a glance out the dangling driver's door. Guard knelt beside Tackle's mangled body. Teresa lowered the .38.

The rear view mirror revealed ridged metal buildings with gable roofs, most about the size of the barn. The upper walls and roof of one more building rose above the others. LEDs lit graveled drive lanes.

Garage doors in three of the smaller buildings rolled up. Interior lighting silhouetted men running to pickup trucks, rifles in their hands. The first pickup raced forward, four male figures silhouetted inside. Moments later, two more pickups joined the chase.

Time to shed the cuffs. Stone writhed over the console and between the front seats, like a submerged escape artist struggling for air. The truck rattled down the gravel lane. Each bump slammed him against the seats. Outside, dust billowed from the wheels of the three pickups, clouding the headlight beams of the trailing two. Enough light came through to reveal the lead pickup's driver wrenching a bucking steering wheel. Getting closer each moment–

Stone stumbled onto the back bench seat. He sat upright and groped behind him. The loop to flip up the bench seat, where was it? Acid burned his throat. The loop should be right here. Here? Come on, where–

There. He hooked sweaty fingers into the loop and pulled. He lifted his rump off the seat and his arms tugged at their sockets. The bench seat flipped forward. The edge dug into his calves.

He sat on the rim of the underseat compartment. Leaned back, groped. His fingers found hard plastic, traced distinctive lines. The rotary cutter. Top of the unit toward the rear, the switch. Slide it. The motor keened. The diamond-edged cutting disc spun at ten thousand RPM in its molded recess. He pulled his hands as wide apart as the cuffs allowed, bent his wrists, lowered the chain toward the diamond edge.

The truck washboarded across the cattle guard. Stone's hands slipped through the air. The cutting disc growled through the metal of the right wristpiece, vibrating his hand. Sparks pricked the bare skin of his forearm.

He jerked his hands away. The cab stank of hot metal. He lowered the chain toward the cutting disc once more. The truck turned left, the broken driver's door swaying. The rotary cutter sliced through the chain.

Relief bathed Stone from the inside. He pulled his hands in front of his body, eyed the gouge in the right wristpiece. An incomplete cut into the metal. No blood. Lucky.

Headlights suddenly glared in the rear view mirror. The brightest they'd been for the entire chase. The men driving the pursuing pickups outperformed Stone's autopilot.

A rifle barked once, somewhere behind him.

Forget the unchained bracelets. He most needed free motion of his feet. He lifted the rotary cutter from its recess and cut the chain between his ankles. His thumb slid the power switch off. He dropped the cutter and scrambled over the console into the driver's seat. His hands and feet slid into position at the wheel and pedals, practiced moves honed almost to instinct. The crunching sound of tires on gravel, and a fine dust of motes reflective in his pursuers' headlights, came through the dangling door.

"Full manual, now!"

The steering wheel jostled in his hand. He mashed the accelerator pedal to the floor. The truck surged forward, gravel rattling under the wheels, billows of dust clouding the trailing headlights in the mirrors. He got further from them with each second. Back and forth he serpentined, a random pattern to deny the riflemen easy aim. On either side of the road, steel fence posts blurred by, the barbs on the wire strands invisible with his speed and the moonless night.

He topped a rise, his rump lifting off the seat. Ahead, a double-headed arrow on a yellow sign glowed in his headlights. The gravel ended at a paved road. Not the highway to the wormhole. "Turn left," the truck said.

"Got it." He looked both ways. No headlights visible in either direction on the paved road. He veered to the right side of the gravel road. The best line for the turn. How fast could he go without the back wheels slipping?

Find out–

He lifted his foot a fraction off the accelerator and turned left. A glimpse of stop sign to the right, a brick pillar in the corner of the field to the left. His left front wheel left the gravel for a moment, then the edge of the pavement punched it, slamming Stone's head toward the ceiling. He pressed the accelerator pedal down to finish the turn and the back wheels slid to the right, rustling gravel onto the paved road, heading for a drainage ditch on the far side.

He eased his foot off the pedal. Nudged the wheel to the right. Four tires gripped the pavement. Go!

Pedal slammed down, he took a breath. A glance at the nav screen showed two miles to the wormhole highway. The map told him he currently traveled on a Kovar Road.

A glare appeared in the rear view mirror. The lead pickup had reached the pavement, but took the turn much slower than Stone. It accelerated after him. The second pickup tried the turn at higher speed and skidded just like Stone, then overcompensated. Amateur driver. The second pickup's back end fell into the ditch, dragged the front end in after it. Headlights stabbed uselessly into the sky. One down.

Stone held the pedal to the floor. The speedometer needle crept up. 90, 95, 100, 105. Air roared over the dangling driver's door and through Teresa's bullet holes. Two sets of headlights remained about a quarter of a mile behind him.

A grin split his lower face. Teresa's cronies played his game of action. Amateurs up against a man who knew in his bones how to play. And win. His truck followed the curves and elevation changes in the road as if it interfaced directly with his brain.

Suspended from taut wires, a red light blinked above the intersection with the wormhole highway, supplementing a stop sign aimed Stone's way. To the left, a blocky sedan on the wormhole highway drove slowly toward the intersection.

"Is this a four-way stop?" he asked the truck.

A chill down the inside of his chest told him the answer before the truck did. "No," said the truck, voice bland as ever. "Cross traffic does not stop."

A glance gave Stone's mind the distances and speeds he needed. He kept the pedal to the floor and crossed into the left lane. Even if the blocky sedan prepared to turn right, he should make it.

He stomped the brake, steered for the apex of the corner, then mashed the accelerator. The dangling door thumped against the fender, then back against the door post. The sedan's headlights blazed like a binary star in his mirrors, insanely close. Brakes squealed behind him. His truck surged away. The speedometer reached 120. The sedan's headlights receded into tiny, squared-off discs as he continued along the highway to the wormhole.

Three-eighths of a mile behind Stone, two pickups swerved around the sedan as if it stood still.

Stone kept the pedal to the floor. With every glance in his mirrors, the lead pickup's headlights seemed brighter and larger. If he stopped at the outbound checkpoint, he'd be a sitting duck, answering ITB security questions while Teresa's cronies centered his head in their rifle sights.

There was another way. It would blow his cover–

Better that than end up dead.

UN operative to all local ITB personnel, he subvoked. *Demand highest priority access to wormhole, auth code 638754523.*

Hours seemingly crawled by. Ninety seconds, in reality, for ITB to validate his code. "Wormhole ops here. Roger that."

Lead vehicle only. Two trailing vehicles are hostile.

The truck crested a roll in the ground. A mile ahead, spotlights resolved the checkpoint's guardhouse and barriers. A band of blue set at ground level three-fourths of a mile beyond the checkpoint writhed with the massive, chained energies of the wormhole. Night in Texas, apparently–the hemisphere of Earthly sky inside the wormhole remained as black as the moonless night of Freeland.

Gentle descent bumped the speedometer to 122. The pickups' headlights crested the roll in the ground, further behind than a few seconds earlier. Ahead, ITB personnel ran to the checkpoint barriers. The red-and-white gates lifted like barber poles coming to attention. Stone took a breath, his deepest since the truck punched open his holding pen. The rustle of tires on the pavement, and wind over and around the dangling door, seemed almost restful, like traffic on the FDR turning into white noise as he readied for his solitary bed.

Stone blinked and shook his head. Stay focused. Something could still go wrong.

Two hundred yards from the checkpoint, he pounded the brake pedal. All four antilocks pulsed. He had enough control to weave across the two lanes and hopefully spoil the aim of any riflemen in the pickups.

At thirty miles an hour, he slalomed past the barriers. He caught an indelible glimpse of an ITB security guard, mouth gaping at Stone's speed. The driver's door clanged against a barrier, hard enough to slam the door frame and bounce back. Then the barriers fell behind him. He accelerated up to sixty. Only an empty lane of fresh asphalt lay between him and the wormhole.

Go through. Report to Gray. Let a commando team take care of Teresa, the rest of the Benavides family, and their allies.

The mirrors showed the two pickups halted outside the barriers. A semicircle of ITB security guards, postures showing a readiness to draw and fire, focused on the pickups. Teresa's cronies wouldn't stop him.

Stone blinked. How long would a commando team need to act? Too long. Teresa would destroy the evidence before the commando team could arrive.

"Automatic mode," he told the truck over the road roar. He unbuckled and twisted his torso between the front seats. He yanked open the storage cubby, reached for the flare gun.

Two hundred meters to the ramp into the wormhole. Close enough to see truncated Earthly constellations in the Texas night sky. "Slow down!"

Stone grabbed the handle above the driver's door with his left hand and leaned out. Wind whipped his hair toward his face. Still a clear enough view of the ITB checkpoint. He aimed and fired out of long practice. The heavy flare streaked out of the tube on a flat trajectory toward the checkpoint. He returned to the driver's seat and put his hands on the wheel. "Manual mo–"

A glare erupted in the mirrors. Stone squinted, turned the headlights off, and yanked the wheel to the right. His truck jostled off the pavement and onto bare ground. Sprangletop tufts, nearly white in the flare's overexposure lashed at the grill and wheel wells.

The flare should have dazzled everyone at the checkpoint, friend and foe alike. But their night vision would recover before long. Stone pressed the accelerator and the truck bounced along. The wheel jumped from side-to-side against his hands but he kept it aimed left of center. The black matte equilibrator ring swallowed the flare's light. Stone drove on around the wormhole, veering closer to the equilibrator ring. The flare faded and the ring shadowed the jumbled ground, plunging Stone and his truck into darkness.

He stopped, shifted into park. The only hint of illumination came from a faint wash of sky from the ITB checkpoint's spotlights, rippling with wormhole distortion.

His grin returned, splitting open his lower face. He laughed then, deep from his gut.

Why should a commando team have all the fun?

CHAPTER 13

n the shadow of the equilibrator ring, lit only by the glowing nav screen, Stone cut through the bracelets and anklets still around his limbs. He twisted between the front seats and pulled a cable tie from the storage bin, then lashed the front and rear doors on the driver's side to the central pillar. He rolled up the windows till their edges pinched the cable tie against the opening. Out the passenger door he went and unscrewed the Texas license plates, front and back. His truck might pass as a local to a casual glance.

Not with bullet holes through the glass. Feet on the ground, Stone pulled from the storage bin a tube of translucent gray putty. He squeezed the putty into the holes in the windshield and rear window. Gray goop smothered reflections of starlight. By morning, the putty should have cured well enough for the locals to overlook it.

He set off. The truck bumped slowly over the rough ground, where tufts of sprangletop and other grasses looked like gray-black blobs in the starlight. Shock absorbers hissed, yet the bumps still rattled his spine.

A big enough hole could snare a wheel. Or fracture an axle.

A glance at the nav screen showed two miles of open ground before a gravel track between ranches.

He looked up. Braked. Even at its dimmest, the nav screen far outshone the night sky's thousand stars. A salmon-pink rectangular afterimage washed out the details of the ground ahead.

Stone shifted to park. "Nav screen and internal lights off."

The truck's bland voice hesitated. "Are you certain?"

"Off. Now. Or I'll file a complaint with your manufacturer."

"You're certain. Complying." The nav screen winked out. The instrument cluster faded into darkness. Stone shut his eyes, blinked them open, rinse and repeat.

Stone's night vision returned. The terrain in front of the truck resolved enough to tell whether the darkest patches were the thick shadows of grass tufts or sizable holes. He shifted into drive and kept his foot off the accelerator. Sprangletop brushed roughly against the truck's undercarriage.

Thirty minutes later, he climbed out of the cab with the rotary cutter. In front of the truck, the barbs of a wire fence glinted in starlight. Beyond the fence, the gravel track was a light gray slash against the darker gray of grass-colored ground.

Stone sliced through five strands of barbed wire. The diamond-edged disc keened, flinging sparks brighter than any overhanging star. Cud-chewing cattle in a field on the other side of the road ignored him. A sweeping look at the horizon showed rolling terrain and clumps of trees, free of the straight lines of constructions and the steady glow of LEDs. With each cut, the wires twanged, coiling toward the nearest steel fence posts.

Stone drove carefully through the gap in the fence, then down and up a drainage ditch. Gravel crunched under his tires, welcoming him back to something resembling a road.

He parked. "Internal lights and nav on." The vehicle complied. Stone swiped at the nav screen. Take the track to a paved road, turn right, go six miles. Right again on a dirt road just after a low-water bridge. Park near a clump of trees, then a mile and a half on foot to discover the secret hidden in Teresa Benavides' machine shop.

Stone turned on the headlights and shifted into self-driving mode. The truck crunched along the gravel track, alone in a bubble of head-lights like a submersible craft in deep ocean. When he reached the paved road, the truck picked up speed. Wind whistled through the slivers of windows wedged open by the cable tie.

The headlights dimmed themselves once, a courtesy to a pickup truck coming the opposite direction. His shoulders tensed. He squinted against the oncoming headlights. Through the headlight glare, he glimpsed a young couple, faces mashed together in heavy kissing while their vehicle roared past Stone. He shook out the tension in his arms as the couple's taillights in his mirrors shrank to dots like twinned red stars.

The low-water bridge was a curbed concrete deck poured over a corrugated steel culvert. A meandering line of live oaks roughly perpendicular to the road marked the now-dry gully running to the culvert. Four hundred yards further, up a mild slope, the truck turned right onto the dirt road. The headlights panned over a pillar of pale brick, two feet on a side and six feet tall, where barbed wire fences along the intersecting roads came together. A ranching brand, an underlined *Ko*, flashed by Stone's eye.

The dirt road ran through a gap in the line of live oaks. On the left, a tree with a crown fifty feet across curled branches down to almost brush the gravel on the road's verge.

"Manual mode." Stone cut the headlights and rolled off the road. The curling branches scratched at his truck's roof as he drove under cover. He parked and dug into the supply kit for matte-black facepaint, high-gain night-vision goggles, and an infrared-reflective poncho folded up in a clear plastic pouch smaller than Gray's old-fashioned smartphone. His fingers smeared facepaint across his cheeks and forehead. He slipped the goggles and poncho into his pocket. IR reflectiveness would make the poncho a sauna if he wore it all the way to the target site. Lastly, he tucked the snub-nosed revolver inside his waistband at the small of his back.

With an extra push against the live oak's swooping limbs, Stone opened the front passenger door. He went around the truck, shone his penlight on knotty roots bursting out of the ground, on the tree's trunk grown into barbed wire strands.

The Jezhek persona stirred in artificial muscle memory. Midway between the oak's trunk and the nearest fencepost, he held one strand down, bent at the waist, and slipped through. One barb snagged at his polo's sleeve, but his free hand easily released it.

Stone ducked under the oak's outermost branches. His implantable put a maroon arrow over the next rise, pointing down at his destination hidden in a valley. Alphanumerics in a matching shade of deep red gave a distance of 2400 yards. He set off. His legs strode through tufted grass and insects frantically hopped away, like particles from the bow of a warp drive ship. He watched for motion and sensors, but saw none in the starlight. Cool air filled his lungs. Almost restful, and impending action brought out a smile. So why did a sour feeling churn in his gut?

She's a good country girl, the Jezhek persona said. *Protecting her people is her only crime. And we're going to kill her for it.*

Stone sniffed out a breath. No, Teresa's only crime was opposing the UN. But he wouldn't go out of his way to kill her. Not even for capturing and nearly liquidating him. All part of the game. She'd almost sacked him, but he'd scrambled just in time....

He stopped at the foot of the rise screening his destination. Only two hundred yards between him and Teresa's workshop. A barbed wire fence shimmered in the gloom atop the rise, about fifty yards away. The fence's posts could mount cameras, mics, and other sensors impossible to see from this distance in starlight.

On the other side of the rise, men shouted above the deep hum of a heavy truck's motor. A rhythmic bleeping, likely the truck's backup warning indicator, cut through the night.

Stone dropped to his belly. Ground as hard as crumbly concrete poked at him in a dozen places. He slipped the night-vision goggles from his pocket, unfolded them, put them over his eyes. *Max gain,* he subvoked to his implantable, and it relayed the command to the goggles.

The rise became a dull haze under a night sky of grayer green. Sparks flashed, perhaps insects or artifacts of the goggles' high gain. Against the sky's backdrop, a set of fluorescent green dots glowed like tiny LEDs. No flash or flicker. Bright green, in a line about five feet above the ground and about fifty feet apart.

No matter how energy efficient Teresa's mics and cameras might be, every electronic device she could fabricate on a backwater world like Freeland would vent enough waste heat to see.

He pulled out the IR-reflective poncho. Despite the poncho's flexible pouch, a crinkle still sounded in the cool night. At his distance, Teresa's mics should miss it. He slipped the poncho over his head and down to his upper thighs, crawling into it like a snake molting in reverse. He pulled the hood over his scalp and crawled up the slope, elbows and knees pulling him forward.

Smells of rocky soil and hardy grass flooded his nose. Sweat trickled between Stone's skin and the snub-nosed revolver. More sweat crept through his eyebrows.

You're going to crawl through cow manure–

No you won't. The rancher's leaving this field to grow back before he'll let cattle graze it again. The Jezhek persona turned scolding. *Though you deserve a faceful of manure for what you want to do to Teresa and the others.*

Stone kept his gaze on a spot along the fence line halfway between two of Teresa's observation devices. Cover stories would get a ton of negative feedback when he returned to headquarters.

He reached the fence. Barbed wire strands stretched above his head. To left and right, three yards away, infrared from the workshops reflected off fence posts.

A thought clamped on his throat. A colony world wouldn't have ultraminiature devices, but a UN turncoat might.

Sweat gushed into his armpits. What the hell were you thinking? Reconnoitering with inferior equipment and no plan?

Quiet, Jezh–

Not Jezhek. Some deep part of his own mind questioned him.

You let Teresa seize the initiative and came within five minutes of getting shot in the back of the head–

He inhaled for focus. Having come this far, he would be less visible observing with his belly on the ground than retreating across an open field. A fast thrumming beat resonated in him.

Copy my optic and auditory nerve inputs, he subvoked. The same transcranial stimulation transceivers feeding data overlays into his vision could copy neural traffic between his retinas and his brain, and function comparably for his auditory system.

His implantable put a red triangle and a green microphone icon in the lower left corner of his sight, latitude and longitude in the lower middle, and a timestamp in the lower right.

Stone shoved the night vision goggles up his forehead, then lifted his head just enough to look between the ground and the lowest strand of barbed wire at the scene downslope.

A dozen boxy structures of sheet metal, laid out haphazardly around gravel driveways. LEDs glowed dimly over rolled-down doors. Light flooded out of an open passageway about twenty feet by twenty in the largest building, perhaps thirty-five feet to the peak of a gable roof. Garage? Barn? A small plane could use it as a hangar. The nose and cab of a tractor-trailer poked out the opening. The light revealed the reversed circle B logo of Benavides' trucking company on the heavy truck's driver's door.

Hitched to the truck, a flatbed trailer parked in the hangar, its rear end hidden from view. The flatbed held a red steel shipping container, of the kind visible on cargo vessels rolling into the New Jersey docks.

Stone frowned. Shipping containers opened at the back, not the top. Not this one. Two hinged metal plates running lengthwise made up the shipping container's top. The near plate slumped against the shipping container's sidewall, and shadows darkened the sliver of interior visible to Stone.

A whine sounded inside the hangar. An object floated into view, swathed in canvas and chained to a ceiling-mounted hoist. The object's print against the canvas suggested a long slab atop a central pillar, the pillar mounted on a broad base. The object presumably would fit into the shipping container, but barely.

The hoist centered the object over the shipping container, then lowered it. A man inside the shipping container raised his hands into Stone's view and guided the object into position. Metal clanged, the sound of clasps locking the object's base onto the shipping container's floor.

The men pulled the chains free of the object. The hoist rose, pulling the dangling chains up and away with a faint tinkle. More pulling, and the canvas slithered over the upper slab and down, out of Stone's view.

Slab, hell.

Six tubes bolted together, side by side. The nose cones and payload canisters of missiles poked out of each tube.

Despite the sweat clinging to his body, a chill stippled Stone's face. Forget rifles to wage guerrilla warfare against UN forces coming through the wormhole.

Teresa's family sought to destroy the wormhole itself.

Distant shouts passed among the men inside the hangar. Along the sides of the flatbed, men raised metal poles with flat flanges on the upper ends. The men shoved the metal plates up, past vertical. The plates dropped with a massive clang rattling out of the hangar opening and up the rise toward Stone.

A yellow motion against the red background of the shipping container caught Stone's eye. Teresa strode into view. Her gaze reflected off the big rig's side view mirror, like a laser reflecting at the driver. She chopped the air with her hand, *go go go*. Her lips moved, but distance muffled her voice.

The tractor-trailer rolled forward, down the gravel driveway. The shipping container turned a plain red face to Stone. Dust caked the license plate on the flatbed. The tractor-trailer drove past a sheet metal structure that abutted a barbed wire fence and turned a wall of four alcoves, shadowed by starlight, toward a field. One of those alcoves had been his makeshift holding cell.

No matter now. The tractor-trailer rolled down the lane Stone followed in his escape an hour earlier. He remembered the stick-on vehicle trackers tucked into his truck's supply cubby and mouthed *Dammit* at the dwindling shipping container. In the thirty minutes or more it would take him to return to his truck and set off in pursuit, the tractor-trailer could be dozens of miles away.

Or it could park a mile from the wormhole and fire its ordnance at the equilibrator ring.

Fools. If they destroyed the equilibrator ring, the wormhole would destroy itself in a burst of gamma rays vaporizing a swath of land twenty miles long and five wide. The hangar and other buildings in front of him would turn into an irradiated haze of gaseous iron and alloy metals. Hell, Svoboda City would disintegrate, killing half the planet's people in an instant. Fallout would blanket thousands of square miles, condemning half the planet's surviving population to radiation sickness or cancer.

That's why ITB never laid equilibrator rings on their side on Earth.

The tractor-trailer's taillights disappeared. Stone's lips pressed together. Did Teresa know what damage she would unleash if her missile strike succeeded?

Stone returned his watch to Teresa. She strode back into the hangar to her uncle Thomas. A brief conversation–mostly her, accented with wide gestures. Her uncle made one terse reply and nodded. Teresa turned and barked orders at two young men strolling by.

At Teresa's orders, men scurried around the hangar and a pickup backed in through the opening. Burly arms hefted barrels into the pickup's bed. The hangar's LEDs lit up skull-and-crossbones stickers and the colored diamond shapes of hazard icons on the barrels. Missile propellant, perhaps, or the raw materials of the missiles' explosive payloads.

Stone let out a breath. She removed evidence from the site. She feared a UN strike team raid in response to Stone's intel before the missile launcher destroyed the wormhole. He had some time to find the tractor-trailer and stop her plan.

How much time?

As she passed into and out of the slice of the hangar's interior Stone watched from his vantage point, he eyed her firm figure, took note of her demeanor commanding the men around her. So young. So absurdly, naively confident, even her uncle Thomas yielded to her.

Thoughts rushed together in Stone's mind. She would want an extra symbolism. Why simply destroy the wormhole, when she could kill the heads of government of two UN member nations in the process?

She knew Yadav and Deshmukh's ETAs. Tomorrow, local time, 0500. He subvoked. His implantable popped a countdown timer into his vision. Stark blue-white numerals ticked down. 16:58:57, 16:58:56, 16:58:55...

Nine hours to stop Teresa from destroying the wormhole. A smirk tightened his cheeks. Simple. Find the tractor-trailer with the red shipping container.

Puzzle pieces slid into place. Stone's smirk reached his eyes. He didn't need to tail the tractor-trailer to find it. Instead, he would ask the owner of this ranch.

CHAPTER 14

Kopachek Street ran from downtown Svoboda City up the curves of a low, sprawling hill. The villas of most of the colony's wealthiest citizens hugged the hill's contours or perched atop gully-carved slopes. For long stretches of the street, the massed foliage of live oaks formed a dense barrier to sight, obscuring both iron fences and automated gates, coming together so thick over the street to blot most of the sky's pre-dawn glow.

But not completely. To the left, Stone glimpsed the gate he sought. *Photo,* he subvoked to his implantable. Down the block, he cut the headlights and parked, with the driveway coming out of the target gate in his mirror.

He subvoked a command. A window popped into view, showing the image captured from his optic nerves. A spotlight on the ground lit up the house number, float-mounted on a pale brick pillar. The number matched the public record. A closed gate of fluted iron rods stood in a track and bore a scripted *K*.

Not Ko-bar, but further confirmation of who lived within.

Another subvoked command fed a map of Svoboda City into his optic nerves. He eyed the shortest path from the villa to the head office of Kovar Construction. His implantable downloaded local traffic data and confirmed Stone's read. In about an hour, Steve Kovar would turn right out of his driveway to go to the office.

Stone swung his truck around to face Kovar's gate. Lowered the window. Powered off the motor. He pulled a slap bracelet from the supply cubby and shoved it into his left trouser pocket. He subvoked for five minutes, dictating an update to Gray. *Send,* he told his wearable.

A whoosh sounded in his ears, then left him with silence. He slouched, watching Kovar's gate with lidded eyes. Time to wait.

Nothing new. He'd spent hundreds of hours on stakeouts, mostly in worse locations than this. A bird chirped amid the oak canopies, *twi-twe-twu twi-twe-twu tw-tw-tw-tw-tw-twu,* and a cool breeze rustled the leaves. A blonde with a lined, middle-aged face jogged by on scrawny legs, reflective stripes running up skintight black yoga pants. She glanced Stone's way with as little interest as his parents had glanced at workmen wrangling squads of maintenance robots. Freeland's sun rose somewhere behind him, its rays dyeing the cloudless sky above pale blue, then azure.

Less than eight hours before Teresa would devastate everything around Stone except the sky.

Around 0445, a rattle came from Kovar's gate. Stone sat up and touched the power button. The trunks and swooping branches of the live oaks dappled his view of a long black sedan and the gate rolling open along its track.

The sedan came through the gate and paused at the end of the driveway. It turned right, away from Stone. The rear license plate matched Kovar's.

"Manual mode," Stone told the truck. He stomped the accelerator. The tires screeched and he raced down the middle of the street. In the rear seats of the black sedan, narrow eyes in a pudgy face turned toward Stone's passage.

Stone yanked the steering wheel to the right and slammed the brakes. Tires shrieked on both his truck and Kovar's sedan. He scrambled out the front passenger door and drew the snub-nosed revolver before his feet landed on the pavement. His gaze pierced the windshield and over the headrests of the rear-facing seats at the front of the sedan's cabin.

Kovar's mouth hung open and his double chin wobbled. His eyes, now wide, tracked the muzzle of Stone's revolver.

Next to her father on the rear seat, Kovar's daughter pushed herself against the door. Thick glass muffled her scream.

Complication. Dammit. Stone stalked to the left-side door, grabbed the handle. Locked. He took his off hand from the revolver and gestured *up*.

Kovar's hands fluttered like drunk birds. He frowned, mouthed *Jezhek?* Then he blinked, twice, and his wits returned to his face. Though barely audible to Stone, Kovar's face showed he shouted the word "Open!"

The door popped an inch away from the sedan. Stone flung the door wide. The girl screamed again and her unmuffled voice pierced the quiet morning.

Stone put his head and gun hand into the cabin. "Quiet. Quiet! Or I put a bullet in your father!"

Kovar laid his flabby arm across his daughter's abdomen. The girl's screams faded into fast and shallow breaths, giddy with panic.

"Hands together in front of you," Stone said to Kovar.

Kovar nodded. The flesh of his face quivered. He raised his arms and touched the insides of his wrists to each other. Revolver in hand and eyes on Kovar, Stone made a sharp motion with his left hand. The slap bracelet thwacked against Kovar's wrists and wrapped around them. Stone thumbed the lock button and a magnet clamped the slap bracelet in place.

Stone backed out of the sedan's doorway. "Both of you, come with me." He gestured with the revolver toward his truck. "Quiet. Casual. Hands in my sight."

The girl spoke softly. "Where are you taking us?"

"Quiet. Get in my truck and I won't have to hurt you."

"Do as he says," Kovar muttered. He levered himself off the seat with his stumpy legs, and got to a standing position on the street without falling over. The girl came next, gripping the door frame with white knuckles before climbing out.

Stone held his revolver close to his belly, moved the muzzle just enough to herd Kovar and his daughter to his truck's rear passenger door. "Pull it open," Stone told the girl.

She nodded, eyes doe-like in obedience. Stone breathed a little easier. Her presence might work for him—

Tires whispered on pavement. In the corner of his eye, a sporty red coupe rolled behind Stone from right to left. A glance showed blond hair framed a lined face dominated by wide eyes and gaping mouth.

Cold dread washed down the inside of his chest. The woman in the red coupe could call the local police before Stone could stop her.

He refocused on Kovar and the girl, gestured at the open door with the revolver. "Get in, both of you. Now!"

Kovar's daughter scrambled in, then reached back for her father's soft hands. With the girl's help, Kovar climbed into the truck. Stone slammed shut the rear passenger door and opened the front door. He stepped his left foot onto the running board and said to the truck, "Turn us around and drive up the street."

The truck backed into a turn as Stone entered the cabin. Forward gear and acceleration Stone used to pull shut the door. He went sideways and backside-first over the center console and to the driver's seat, his gaze tracing routes on the nav screen up Kopachek Street and out of Svoboda City.

In the mirror, the girl clung to her father, her half her face buried against her father's shoulder. Lank hair partially obscured one frightened eye.

Stone stared at her mirrored eye, then shifted his gaze to Kovar. "Lie down and stay out of sight," he said. "If you want to live."

Kovar's jowls wobbled with a nod. He stretched out, on his side facing forward, his bulk filling most of the seat. The girl knelt in the cramped space behind the driver's seat. Her hands clutched her father's.

Stone tucked his revolver inside his waistband at the small of his back. "Manual mode," he told the truck. He pushed the accelerator down and the pistol dug against his back. He glanced again at the nav. Svoboda City might be a small town, but he still faced miles of public roads, crowded with morning commuters and overwatched with traffic cameras, before he could get into the countryside.

His eyes perked. He didn't need to get into the countryside. Another glance at the nav screen showed the neighborhood of UN offices and residences lay less than a mile away. If he could reach a UN facility before the local police detained him, he could interrogate Kovar in a garage or a basement under the cover of diplomatic immunity.

Mature oaks raced by as quickly as Stone's thoughts. If he commandeered access a UN facility, he would leave a data trail the UN turncoat could pick up. The turncoat would relay intel about Stone's presence and Kovar's abduction to Teresa and the rest of the rebels. She would move the missile launcher from its overnight destination to one Kovar couldn't reveal under questioning.

Or she'd raid the facility to rescue her–lover?

Kopachek Street formed a Y-intersection with another street coming in from the right, Yaeger Road. His turn toward the UN zone. He braked, hard, and rubber wailed under the quiet oaks. The sound echoed off the brick wall of the corner lot as if it could run a mile or more to the town's main streets.

Stone took a deep breath. The UN turncoat and the Freelander rebels believed he'd gone through the wormhole. Keep an advantage as long as you can.

He gripped the wheel near his lap, below the bottom of the windows. Glanced in the mirror, where Kovar hunkered, eyes shifting and teeth nibbling at his lower lip. The girl whimpered. Minding their place, both of them.

Relay the truck's external cameras to my vision, Stone told his implantable. He shut his eyes. The intersection and the brick wall filled his vision like a video game.

Stone lifted his foot from the brake pedal, leaned back, and continued along Kopachek Street.

In daylight, the molded black alloy of the Ko brand stood sharply against the dun brick pillar at the corner of Kovar Road and the gravel turn-off. Stone opened his eyes and turned right. His truck crunched along the gravel road, riding swells and dips in the rolling, grassy terrain. A half mile to the right, cattle bent their heads to graze. No other mammals in sight.

He took a chance coming here, but only a slight one. Teresa had almost certainly abandoned the site. She might be an amateur, but she'd shown enough talent to play the game well. A shame she could never prove her political reliability. Otherwise she might have a chance to pass the tests at Gray's charm school.

Are you getting soft?

Stone sniffed out a breath. Soft? Him? Hell no. His job would be easier if people like Teresa Benavides would accept the inevitable UN domination of their societies.

As if you want an easy job, the Jezhek persona replied. *You get constant action without consequences. I reckon that's exactly what you want.*

The truck crested a roll in the terrain. A set of brick pillars came into view, flanking a gravel driveway with the Ko-bar logo. Stone eased off the accelerator. Then I can't be getting soft, can I?

He started up the driveway. Steel roofs, dingy gray in full morning light, peeked over a low rise. Stone's gaze flicked closer, from fence-post to fencepost, looking for microphones and cameras. None came to sight.

She'd pulled even evidence suggesting the occupiers of the gray steel buildings had any reason to hide their activities. A very talented amateur.

Stone made another turn. The barn where Tackle and Guard held him captive stood directly in front of him. The roll-up door remained raised. On the far side of the slab, the gate leaned its bent crossbars on the mangled trough.

Use the barn? He'd spent enough time there the previous night. Part of him, too, wanted to see how thoroughly Teresa had cleaned up the hangar. He steered down the main gravel driveway, left wheels in the center and right wheels squeaking on trampled grass. His tires avoided overlapping shallow grooves in the gravel. Tracks of the tractor-trailer's eighteen wheels.

The hangar's main door gaped as if drawing in a deep breath of morning air. Stone drove onto the concrete floor. Bare all the way to the sheet metal walls. A vertical strip of daylight marked a slightly ajar man-sized door in the far left corner. Not even an empty tobacco tin or can of energy drink nestled against the steel girders. Only a few faint reddish-brown streaks discolored the gray slab with six-inch squares and circles two feet in diameter. Wear and tear from heavy equipment recently moved out of the hangar.

Stone powered down the truck and crawled over to the front passenger seat. A moment later, his feet hit the concrete. Birds chirped outside. He inhaled deep into his torso and caught a trace of oils, solvents, and metals.

He pulled open the rear passenger door. "Get out."

The girl climbed down the running board on trembling legs. Eyes wide, her head swiveled to take in her surroundings. Her face remained blank of any recognition of the location. Fear could do that.

In the back of the truck, the seats squeaked. Kovar sat up. He looked around the hangar and the skin bunched between his eyebrows. "Why did you bring us here, Jezhek?"

"You'll see. Now get out."

Kovar raised his bound wrists, then leaned toward his daughter. "Stop gawking and help me!"

She turned, shoulders hunched, arms lifted. With her help, Kovar descended to the concrete like a deflating beach ball. Rapid breaths heaved his chest. Up came his bound wrists. Excess cable tie extended from his wrists like some rodent's stiff white tail. "Take this thing off me, will you?"

Stone extended his left hand toward the concrete ten feet from his truck's open door. "Sit over there."

"You said you weren't going to hurt us. My hands are tingling." Kovar looked around and his eyebrows arched. "My men aren't around to help us escape. What the hell did you do with them?"

This time, Stone gestured with the snub-nosed revolver. "Sit. Over. There."

Kovar flinched. He waddled where Stone bade. His daughter went at his side and gripped his forearms to help him sit. He squatted; her arms trembled and she uttered little gasps. His arms slipped free and he landed with a thud on his padded backside. "Dammit, I need you to help me!"

"I'm sorry, daddy, I didn't mean to..." Imminent tears edged her voice.

Stone went to the truck's open passenger door. He switched the revolver to his left hand and watched Kovar and the girl.

"–don't you dare cry on me. Keep your head on straight. Dammit, listen to me!" Kovar's voice echoed off the sheet metal walls.

Gaze still on his captives, Stone's right hand flipped open the underseat storage and picked out the item he wanted. A stiff net, wadded up against a housing containing a battery pack and transceiver.

"Daddy, please, I'm sorry, please, don't shout–" The girl hunched over and sobbed.

He strode toward Kovar and the girl, snapping the heel of his shoe against the slab with each step. He gripped the housing and shook out the net to its full size and shape, a rough hemisphere about the size of a human cranium. The net's rigid strands held the shape as pinpoint LEDs glowed green and diagnostic texts scrolled up Stone's vision. Ready to go.

Kovar spoke with a stern edge. "I told you, do not cry on me–"

"Quiet," Stone said. "And be more grateful toward your daughter. Without her, you'd have never met Teresa Benavides."

Kovar's face turned pale. His daughter's sobs lessened. She looked up through red-rimmed eyes. "What does he mean, daddy?"

Jowls wobbling, Kovar said, "He, I, I don't–"

"I mean she's his lover."

The girl's mouth fell open. Her eyes widened like a rabbit's seeing a snake. She whispered, "Daddy?"

"Jezhek is lying!" Kovar's desperate voice echoed off the sheet metal walls.

Stone took one step closer, crowding both Kovar and his daughter. "Someone is lying." He raised the brain scanner. "This will tell us who."

CHAPTER 15

Stone shoved the scanner onto Kovar's head. Kovar writhed like a confused dog, gaze darting up in a vain attempt to see the scanner helmet.

Stone took three steps back and smirked. *Feed audio of the scanner's analysis output through the truck,* he told his wearable. A cheery, rising *bing-bing-bing* poured from the truck's speakers and out its open doors. In the corner of Stone's vision, a pop-up showed a grayscale 3d map of Kovar's brain. Whiter streaks–electrical currents of brain activity–raced through the map like neon lights in Havana's casino district.

Kovar slumped now, shoulders hunched and eyes turned up toward Stone's revolver. His daughter sat on her knees and hugged herself. Her mousy gaze flicked between the two men with an expression of not knowing which to fear more.

"Your name?" Stone asked Kovar.

"What?"

"Your. Name."

Beady eyes widened, a sign he understood Stone calibrated the scanner. "Steve Kovar."

"Date of birth?"

"11 April 2071."

"Place of birth?"

"Dvorak Hospital, Svoboda City."

Bing-bing rang from the truck's speakers. In Stone's vision, the brain map showed bright green streaks of current. Calibration complete.

"Where are we?" Stone asked.

"I–" Kovar rapidly blinked. "I don't know."

Red blossomed like gunshot wounds in Kovar's frontal lobes. The truck made a *bong*.

Stone angled his revolver, bringing the cylinder into view. The centerfire primers showed dull salmon eyes against the brass cartridges. He then turned a flat stare on Kovar. "I'll ask that again. Where are we?"

Kovar's double chin quivered. "My–my ranch."

A *bing* and bright green.

"Good. What was Teresa Benavides fabricating here?"

"What?"

"I'm asking the questions. You're answering them. What was Teresa Benavides fabricating here?"

Kovar gaped at the revolver muzzle. "I don't know." He breathed raggedly, raised wide eyes to Stone. "I swear, I don't know!"

The brain map showed bright green. *Bing* came from the truck's open doors.

"Did you hear that?" Kovar's voice strained. "I'm telling the truth!"

Stone's eyebrow lifted. Next to impossible this pudgy colonist could fool the scanner. "What did she tell you she was building here?"

"She never said." *Bing*.

"Did you ask?"

"No." *Bing*. Green traces swirled through Kovar's brain map on a route different from his previous answers, sparking red as they went. Truth, taking a detour through evasiveness and self-doubt.

Stone asked, "Why did you allow her to use your ranch's work buildings?"

Kovar dabbed his fat pink tongue over dry lips. "I, it, she asked."

Bing. Kovar's eyes eased shut and tension sagged out of his shoulders.

Time to tighten the screws. "When did you first have sex with Teresa Benavides?"

A sidelong glance at his daughter, then Kovar pulled up his chest. "Never." *Bing.* The green traces sparked red and burrowed deep into the roots of Kovar's brain.

Stone guffawed. His laugh echoed off the rigid metal walls and concrete floor. Now it came clear.

Kovar's tough front collapsed. His daughter cycled a confused gaze between him and Stone.

Stone's laugh grew quieter, but even more mocking. "She wouldn't give her body to a fat man twice her age. Not that she needed to. She played to your longing and you gave her all she asked for." He gestured with the revolver's muzzle toward the hangar's vast interior and the other buildings beyond. "Freedom to work here, with your men, no questions asked. And because you gave her all that, she was never going to put out. You realize that now?"

Kovar hunched forward. He angled his red cheeks away from his daughter.

The girl unfolded her arms. "You want to have sex with someone my age? I went to school with her!"

Kovar turned his shoulders a few more inches away from his daughter. Red spiraled through the brain map before he spoke. "No," he said quietly.

Bong sounded from the truck.

The girl blinked eyes puffy and glistening with tears. "Daddy, how could you!"

"I, honey... his scanner is rigged–"

The girl bawled. Her tears plinked on the concrete slab. Kovar reached his bound hands toward her, drew them back.

Stone stepped back. A dead end spiralling into a domestic drama. Kovar knew nothing about Teresa's missile launcher. Still, he had to ask. "Did you give her access to other buildings you own?"

Kovar turned away from his crying daughter. He looked relieved to have surrendered to Stone. "No." The scanning software confirmed him.

"Did you give her access to other open land?"

"No." Kovar spoke truthfully. No surprise. Teresa would be too shrewd to build her missiles within sight of the UN's airborne eyes.

"Did you–"

In the lower right corner of Stone's vision, a bright red light blinked. A klaxon sounded in his auditory nerves in time with the light.

What? he subvoked.

His wearable fed a hiss to his hearing, indicating a gain turned high on the truck's microphones. Over the hiss came the crunch of tires on gravel. An overlay estimated the sound came from eighty yards up the driveway and approached at five miles an hour.

"Get in the truck," Stone said.

"What? In the truck?" Kovar blinked. His mouth fell open. "I've answered your questions. Don't kill us!"

His daughter swung red raccoon eyes up to Stone's face. She held his gaze for a moment, then shrank back, wailing in the empty hangar.

"No one dies if you get in the truck!" Stone stalked to the girl and grabbed her upper arm. He yanked her to her feet and shoved her toward the truck's open doors.

In his auditory nerves, the tires crunched louder. Now sixty yards away, the approaching vehicle picked up speed.

Not enough time to get hands-bound Kovar into the truck. Stone went to his truck's rear wheel and knelt, facing the rolled-up vehicular door. He raised the revolver, left side of the barrel against the rigid plastic over the brake and turn signal lights, and aimed where a car would hold its passengers' heads.

He heard the crunch of tires in his ears, now. Following the last curve of the driveway. The approaching vehicle would cross into view any moment. Stone held his breath to steady his aim.

The front end of a pale green sedan rounded the corner. The car belonging to the keyhole kop.

How the hell had she found him? And what did she want? His eye narrowed over the revolver's sights.

The hangar's open garage door now framed the entire sedan. The windows showed only upholstered seats and an unobstructed view across the cabin to the country landscape beyond.

Where was Fredriksen?

A chill rippled over Stone. The personnel door behind him–

He snapped his head around. Caitlyn Fredriksen stood on the far side of Kovar, feet in soft-soled shoes planted on the concrete, and both hands on an ITB standard issue pistol–sleek and matte-black–aimed at Stone's torso.

"I don't expect a UNICA agent to try to shoot me," she said. She shook her head as she spoke and her blond ponytail swayed. "But even so, slowly put the revolver on the floor."

Stone's mind raced. He kept the revolver pointed toward the rolled-up garage door. "Oona-what?"

Fredriksen angled her head, cocked a disapproving eyebrow. "Does Gray think I'm an idiot? Or do you?"

CHAPTER 16

tone squinted at her. "Who the hell is Gray?"

"That answers my question." Fredriksen's pistol remained steady, a splinter of midnight poised to pierce Stone's chest. "Cut the crap. The moment we realized what kind of colony existed on Freeland, our Earth offices started monitoring Czech and Slovak ethnic and cultural groups. Then PACSCuPS–that's the group Jasper Jezhek supposedly works for, remember?–appeared out of nowhere. Out of nowhere, but with twenty years of fraudulent archives in the worldweb and non-profit organization paperwork filed in Austin and Washington, D.C. Only UNICA could root a cover story that deeply." She nodded at Stone's revolver. Her agate eyes flashed. "Put your weapon down and let's talk."

Stone lowered his revolver. A whimper came from the truck's open door. Kovar's daughter. Kovar himself remained seated on the concrete, bound hands in front of him, face wobbling as he turned from Stone to Fredriksen, gaze groping for understanding.

"In front of them?" he asked.

Fredriksen took her left hand off her sleek black pistol and reached for the small of her back. She pulled out an off-white, plastic pistol reminiscent of a child's toy. She kept her gaze on Stone and pointed the toy weapon at Kovar. A plastic click, a puff of air. Kovar lifted his hands toward a tiny dart on his cheek. For a second, his eyes grew more confused, then drooped. The rest of his body slumped down to the floor. His upper arm pillowed his pudgy, sleeping face.

She stepped closer to Kovar's daughter and fired another sedative dart.

Stone rose to his full height. The rubber and dirt smells from the nearby tire remained strong. Five yards across the concrete, drool pooled in the corner of Kovar's slack mouth.

"They still heard what you said earlier," Stone said.

Fredriksen lowered her pistol to her side. She fixed her hazel eyes on him. "The drug cocktail in the dart will disrupt their memories of the last six hours. We can talk."

"You first. How did you find me?"

"The Svoboda City surveillance camera network was an easy hack. We watched your truck drive away from the hotel late last night without you in it. Shortly after that, our security detail at the wormhole saw you drive through and vanish in a flash of light. This morning, when the local police channel squawked that a vehicle matching your truck's description was involved in the kidnapping of Kovar and his daughter, we launched an airborne drone that tracked you here." She flicked the wrist of her free hand toward the open vehicular doorway behind Stone. "Four thousand meters is nothing to the drone's telephoto lens."

She took a half-step toward Stone. Daylight glittered in her golden eyes. "Now it's your turn. What does Kovar have to do with the Benavides family's plan?"

Stone smiled, lazily, buying time. The UN turncoat might be standing in front of him. Tell her everything he knew, and she could decide to tie off loose ends. Fredriksen could empty the clip of her sleek black pistol before he could pick up and cock, let alone fire, his revolver.

His thoughts shifted. If she were the UN turncoat, she already knew what Teresa had done here... and that Stone knew it too. She might still try to kill him, but not for telling her the truth.

"He let Teresa work on it in this place. He knows nothing beyond that."

Eyebrows arched, Fredriksen said, "You've been on-planet only twenty-hour hours, yet already gathered intel we've missed for months?"

Stone smirked. "Maybe I'm better at tradecraft."

She shifted her weight, set her left fist to her hipbone, elbow jutting out. "Are you now?"

His smirk grew, warming the upper corners of his mouth. "You're pretty when you act indignant. What intel do you have on their plan?"

"Lukas and Teresa Benavides are fabricating rifles and rifle ammunition at their ranch."

"And?"

"They're planning a military operation to overwhelm our security detail at the wormhole and blockade traffic coming from Earth."

"When will you arrest them?"

"We won't."

Stone blinked. "Because—"

"My superiors want the Benavides family to stage their operation. We project they can muster about seventy-five riflemen. They can kill the guards at the wormhole and any civilians caught driving through. That's enough for us to wave a bloody shirt in the General Assembly and Security Council. The Secretary-General would authorize a peace-keeping mission to wipe out all opposition on Freeland."

"A sensible plan. It will lead to disaster if you keep following it."

Creases formed in the creamy skin of her forehead. "What the hell are you holding back?"

Stone blew out a breath. "The Benavides family isn't planning to interdict the wormhole. They're planning to destroy it."

His words rocked Fredriksen back on her heels. A moment later, she blinked her hazel eyes and shook her head as if to fling off her reaction. "Small arms can't do that."

"Six armor-piercing missiles might."

She shook her head again. "We would have picked up evidence of missile construction at the Benavides ranch...." Up went her eyebrows. "They built their missiles here? How do you know?"

"Last night, Teresa, her uncle, and a couple of her goons took me captive."

"A twenty-year old girl got the drop on one of Gray's veteran operatives? Ah. I can guess exactly how." Fredriksen rolled her eyes. "Still believe you're better at tradecraft?"

Stone slowly waggled his head side-to-side. "Don't interrupt. They held me in a livestock pen in another barn on this ranch. By claiming to be working on their side, I bought enough time to call my truck from the city."

"While you were held captive, you saw Teresa and Thomas Benavides working on their missiles?" Skepticism filled her tone.

"I didn't *see* the work, but I heard it. After I escaped and faked the wormhole transit, I drove up a gravel road–" Stone kept his head motionless while his sense of direction swung like a neural network compass needle. He pointed over the bed of his truck at the sheet metal wall. "–that way. Parked under the low branches of an oak and infiltrated cross-country to get a better look."

Fredriksen raised her free hand, palm up. "At what?" Her voice echoed off the hard surfaces of the empty hangar.

"They knew I'd made them. I saw them scrub evidence and evacuate their operation. Want to see the video?"

The muscles in her throat showed a hard swallow. "Send it over."

Stone subvoked to his implantable. In the right edge of his vision, lines of text flickered by and a progress bar rapidly filled with green.

Fredriksen stared at the concrete floor near Stone's feet, a distracted look in her hazel eyes. A sucked-in breath and a wide-eyed glance at Stone told him she'd seen the missile launcher get loaded. Her torso rocked with her next breaths. She collected herself, then sliced her left hand edgewise through the air.

"You've seen enough," Stone said.

Her cheeks looked pale. "Where's that red intermodal container?"

She didn't know about Teresa's missile launcher. Fredriksen wasn't the UN turncoat. Stone let out a breath. "If I knew, I'd be there now."

"Does she know what will happen? The energies released if the wormhole loses equilibrium–"

"Does it matter whether she knows or not?"

Fredriksen touched her fingers to her parted lips. Slowly she shook her head. "Why hasn't she attacked the wormhole already? Is she trying to get clear of the gamma ray burst?"

"She wants to blow the wormhole when Yadav and Deshmukh are coming through."

"Who?"

"Rival heads of government from two UN member states in South Asia. They've called in favors with your bosses and will bull through the wormhole to win political points back home. Their ETA is–" Stone shook his watch down his wrist. A dazzle in the polished black face failed to obscure the arms. "Just over five hours from now."

She squinted at Stone. "How does she know–Yadav and Deshmukh, do I have the names right?–are coming to Freeland?"

If Fredriksen didn't know about the turncoat working in UN operations on Freeland, he would keep at least one UNICA secret. And if she did know about the turncoat, no harm in letting her think he remained in the dark. "I told her," Stone said nonchalantly.

Fredriksen's mouth hung slack for a moment. She shook her head and scowled. "Gray and his damn cowboys."

"Telling her last night means we still have five hours to find her and the missile launcher. And we know where she's going–to within range of the wormhole."

"Which only limits her to dozens of square miles we'll have to search–"

Stone smirked. "Do you want to keep talking or do you want to go find her?"

"Together?"

"Yes, together. If we pool our resources, we're much more likely to find her than if we're hiding intel from one another."

Fredriksen looked thoughtful for a moment, then made one brisk nod. "Deal. First, let's get Kovar and his daughter into your truck and send it to their house."

"I can't dismiss my truck like that."

"Pull Gray's goodie bag out from wherever you hid it. We can't drive your truck around, especially if we have to go into Svoboda City. Every policeman on the planet is looking for that truck and its operator. If the police arrest you for kidnapping, whether I talk your way out or you shoot your way out of their custody, we'll waste too much time."

"Good point." He smirked again. "You're not so bad at tradecraft after all."

Her face failed to register his expression. "Let's save the mutual praise until after we stop Teresa Benavides from destroying the wormhole. And half the colony with it."

Stone nodded. He picked up his revolver and tucked it in the back of his waistband, then stepped onto the running board, leaned forward, and climbed into the rear of the cabin. Kovar's daughter lay on her left side across the bench seat, close enough to the edge that her right arm dangled toward the carpeted floorboard. Stone shoved her against the backrest, then flipped up the middle part of the seat. Despite the presence of Kovar's daughter, he lifted the seat far enough to reach his free hand into every spot inside the storage compartment.

"While you're doing that, I'll pull local police cameras for a lead on the red intermodal container."

"Wait. Do the local police know you've cracked their cybersecurity?" He threw the flare gun and the handheld rotary cutter out the truck's open doors; they skidded and clattered on the concrete.

"No."

"Are you certain?" He pocketed a sheaf of cable ties matching the ones binding Kovar's wrists, and a gas torch the size of a marking pen.

"Certain enough. Even if they do know, we're continually pulling data from their cameras. They would only know the red intermodal container is important to us if Teresa Benavides told them."

Stone ripped up the slate-gray foam sculpted with the outlines of equipment. "She wouldn't tell the local authorities. Even if they're sympathetic to her. She's an amateur, but she's talented enough to operate on need-to-know." He tossed chunks of ripped foam at the open doors. A sweep with his free hand revealed only mangled strips of foam clinging to the compartment's straight walls.

He lowered the bench seat. The unconscious girl lay on her back, her mousy lips pursed. Stone pulled her to a seated position, then slid her across the seat to the left side window. Her head lolled back and forth, ending up slumped forward, chin toward her chest.

Stone backed out of the space and jumped to the concrete. He turned and strode toward Kovar's head. "Help me with him."

Fredriksen picked up Kovar's ankles while Stone lifted the man by the armpits. Grunting under most of Kovar's weight, Stone shuffled backward toward the truck's open doors. He searched behind himself with his right foot for the running board, then ducked and pulled Kovar up into the truck's cabin without banging his head or toppling over. He manhandled Kovar into a seated position, then yanked the magnetic resonance net off Kovar's head and climbed out.

Stone shut the truck's doors. *Drive to Kovar's house*, he subvoked to the truck. *Park on the street, then wipe your memory.*

"Sir, are you certain?" The truck's bland voice spoke through his wearable to his auditory nerves.

Completely.

The truck backed toward the open hangar door. Its tires crunched gravel, then slithered over grass as it went around Fredriksen's green sedan.

He looked at Fredriksen. Sweat matted her hair to her temples, darkening it to a medium brown. Her breaths still came slightly raggedly. "They're on their way to Kovar's house," he said. "Have anything from local police cameras."

She gulped a deep breath. "Not yet."

Stone kicked torn foam and spilled items from the storage compartment into a pile on the gray slab. He pulled the gas torch from his pocket and inverted it. While he unscrewed the fuel cap, he said, "While we're waiting, we'll take a run at Lukas Benavides. See what he knows."

Fredriksen shook her head. "We'll get results from police cameras."

Stone drizzled fuel over the pile. The thick smell wrinkled his nose. To think Manhattan smelled like carbon fuels a century ago. "Unless she avoided known camera sites before she unloaded the missile. Or switched containers. Or used a hundred cans of spray paint."

"I ordered the drone to recon around the wormhole. If it sees anything the size of that missile launcher on the move, it'll track it and relay its intel to me. There are also some abandoned bioseeding sites big enough to hide the missile launcher. The drone will check those too."

"Unless Teresa already has it emplaced." His fingers threaded the fuel cap back onto the bottom of the torch. Stone switched gears, gave her a charming smile. "You set two good plans in motion. But a threat against wormhole containment is big enough to call for a third." He held the smile on her an extra moment, then crouched and reversed the torch. He slid the safety and pressed the ignition button. A blue-white flame blazed at the torch's tip. Stone moved it closer to the pile. The drizzled fuel caught fire with a whoosh.

Stone squinted against the heat, then turned off the torch. He angled his head sideways at Fredriksen's green sedan. Over the crackle of popping plastic, he said, "Get in and set the destination for Benavides' ranch."

CHAPTER 17

Twenty minutes later, the green sedan accelerated past the stockyard on Frichville Highway. Recirculated air kept the stockyard's manure stench outside and concentrated the scents of shampooed carpet and Caitlyn's perfume in the sedan's cabin.

They'd switched to first names before climbing into the sedan at Kovar's ranch. *Caitlyn* rolled through his mind much more easily than her surname. He'd forget her given name after this mission, exactly like he'd forgotten women's names passionately whispered at night in the skyscraper-sliced light of Manhattan mornings.

You must be so proud.

Stone pushed the Jezhek persona's judgment away. Focused on the woman across the cabin from him. Caitlyn sat in the left forward seat, arm stretched atop the backrest, narrow nose and hazel eyes aimed at the right side windows. She scowled at passing storage tanks and pipe trees without seeing them.

"Local police cameras have no sign of the missile launcher?" Stone asked.

"No. At least we know they didn't drive through Svoboda City."

Stone called up from his implantable a map. The colony's roads branched and twisted like the neurons of the brain's hemispheres. Continuing the metaphor made the City Bridge in downtown Svoboda City the corpus callosum, the only connection between the halves of the brain. "Depending on who got the contract, UN surveyors could miss another bridge."

"We update our maps twice a week with our own drone recon," Caitlyn said. "There's no bridge."

He remembered shipping containers stacked on transport ships approaching the Jersey docks. "It's unlikely, but can we rule out a barge ferried the missile launcher across the river?"

"Yes. We've hacked into the riverine navigation authority's computer systems. There are only three places where roads come to the riverbank and the river is deep enough for a barge. From registered barge transponders, we know no barge has loitered at those locations after your timestamped video of the missile launcher's departure."

"Anything from your drones?"

"Not yet. The abandoned bioseeding facilities around the wormhole look unoccupied from the air, in visual and radar."

The southeastern outskirts of Svoboda City thinned out, giving way on either side to rolling plains tufted with dark green sprangletop. Augment the terrain's dips with a little shovel work and you could hide a thousand shallow graves. "Looks like we'll have to extract the intel from Lukas Benavides." His tone sounded cool, but he sensed the heat behind his words.

She peered at him. "You want revenge against him because Teresa almost killed you?"

"I want to complete the mission." He held his gaze steadily on her. "If your electronics give us the intel we need in time, great. But if they don't..." He shrugged, rolling his wrists to put his hands into the gesture.

"To extract the intel from Benavides your way, we first have to take Benavides into custody. How do you propose to do that?"

"We park on a side road and infiltrate overland." Stone subvoked to his implantable. It beamed a map to Caitlyn. "I marked a spot where we could partially conceal your car, about two miles from Benavides' house–"

"Two miles on foot, in daylight? Did you pull two chameleoncloth suits out of your truck?"

Stone spoke with more emphasis. "We'll follow terrain contours until we reach the cover of the workshops and barns. Once we get visuals on him, we'll rush the ranch house and extract him."

Caitlyn arched a sculpted brown eyebrow. "*That's* the best plan you've come up with?"

His thoughts came up short. Then Stone laughed. "It's damn weak, I know." A lazy smile filled his face. "But you don't have any better plan."

The light glinted in her hazel eyes. "Yes I do."

"Ha. What?"

She leaned forward. The glint in her eyes intensified. "We'll head up the driveway and knock on his front door."

The green sedan parked itself between the live oak and Benavides' ranch house. The left door popped open. Caitlyn uncrossed her lithe legs and lifted her sleek black pistol from her lap, to a height above the bottom of the sedan's windows.

"That's my cue," Stone said through a sullen mouth. Easy this morning to use the method acting trick of remembering a time he'd felt the appropriate emotion. Just go back eight hours, to being marched out of the hotel by Teresa.

Stone scowled at Caitlyn and climbed out of the sedan. A breeze rustled the live oak's leaves. His gaze drifted over a disguised camera on the tree's trunk as if he didn't see it. The smells of dirt and grass reminded him of the livestock pen at Kovar's ranch.

Caitlyn's shoes padded the ground behind him. "Around the car. Slowly. Hands in sight at all times."

Shoulders hunched, Stone trudged toward the ranch house. Tracks from Caitlyn's sedan now and his truck from the previous afternoon overlapped on the gravel.

"Who the hell are you?"

Stone looked up. Lukas Benavides stood on the path's granite slab closest to the breezeway. He squinted, hat pushed up. Two young men, a few years younger than Guard and Tackle and far too scrawny to play offensive line, flanked Benavides and gripped stamped-metal assault rifles with long curved magazines.

"I'm Jasper Jezh–"

"I'm asking her." Benavides aimed his slitted eyes squarely at Caitlyn. "Well?"

Stone had his back to her, but he could see the glint in her eyes from the tone of her next words.

"I'm the UN official who's been working with you for months," Caitlyn said. "May we go inside?"

The young men blinked and glanced sidelong at Benavides. The older man raised his weathered hand to clam them. To Caitlyn, he said, "I don't know what you're talking about."

"Admirable opsec, Lukas. Part of why I'm glad I've worked with you. Anyway, our agreed plan has gone pear-shaped, for a couple of reasons–" Stone assumed she gestured at him with her sleek black pistol. "–and the clock is so close to zero I had to come straight to you. May we go inside?"

Benavides' eyes narrowed further, then he stepped off the path and hooked his thumb at the ranch house's front door. "Go on in."

One of the scrawny boys led the way. Stone followed him, two yards ahead of Caitlyn's soft footfalls. Inside, the scrawny boy hefted the assault rifle and gave Stone a tough look from ten feet away. Stone hunched his shoulders and showed the boy his open palms. A glance showed the boy didn't have the ruthlessness for this work. Stone could draw the snub-nosed revolver from the back of his waistband before the boy would raise and fire the assault rifle.

If Caitlyn's plan worked, he wouldn't have to.

Caitlyn, the other boy, and Benavides came in from outside. Benavides strode to his leather armchair, waving at the facing sofa. "Sit, both of you."

Stone slumped onto the sofa and gazed at the synthwood floorboards. Caitlyn tucked her black pistol behind her back and took a seat to Stone's left. Benavides eased into his leather armchair, far more spryly than Kovar could have. One of the boys took a standing position behind Benavides, backlit by the windows onto the barns and other outbuildings. The other boy waited behind Stone and Caitlyn.

Caitlyn leaned toward Benavides. "Thank you for meeting with me."

"Mighty glad to meet someone we've worked with so long," Benavides said. The corners of his salt-and-pepper mustache lifted. "From your voice over the phone, I reckoned you were a Frenchman."

Stone's head wanted to snap up. He kept it down and only moved his eyes Caitlyn's way. *He's laying a trap–*

I can tell, Caitlyn replied, subvoking through their implantables to his auditory nerves. "You were listening in without telling me all those times I spoke with Teresa? I thought a Freeland gentleman would have better manners than that."

Benavides bowed his head. "Only once, and I do apologize."

"Accepted," Caitlyn said with a smile that quickly evaporated. "Now let's get down to business."

"Gladly. Lot of business to get down to." Vulnerability softened the horizontal lines of his face. "Do you know where Teresa is?"

Caitlyn sucked in a breath. "I came here hoping you could answer that question for *me*. When did you last see her?"

"Last night, about 1200. Jasper–that isn't his name, is it?"

"One of his many lies to you," Caitlyn said. "His real name is Stone Chalmers. He's an undercover operative for a secret UN agency."

"Chalmers here had just gone back to the city after dinner. Teresa, Thomas, and a couple of my great-grandsons set out after him. What did you tell her?"

Stone stared at the wingtip on Benavides' polished brown boot. He and Caitlyn had discussed everything they knew about the UN turncoat on the drive out Frichville Highway. He had to trust Caitlyn to play the part.

She spoke. "I told Teresa he cheated to pass both your tests of his cover story."

"The UN really can change the DNA in a man's skin." Benavides whistled a falling tone. "Doesn't matter. They went after him to get his original DNA and I haven't heard from her since." The old man showed nut-brown irises in the pronounced whites of his eyes. "Did you kill them, you UN bastard?"

Head up, Stone gave him a cold stare, then sniffed out a breath and turned away.

"Chalmers killed one of your great-grandsons when he escaped from Teresa," Caitlyn said. "Teresa and the other two survived."

"We'll remember him the way we remember the Texans who died at the Alamo." Satisfaction crept into Benavides' voice. "She took a UN spy captive, then, at least for a while. That girl makes me prouder and prouder."

Inside Stone, the Jezhek persona echoed the sentiment, tinged with romantic longing.

Benavides' brow crinkled. "Where did all this happen? Our friends in Svoboda City PD and the rangers would have told me all this, if they knew."

"Teresa and the others took Chalmers to Steve Kovar's ranch."

The crinkles deepened. "Kovar? The fat traitor who wants to get fatter selling out our colony to the UN hordes?"

"It turns out..." A pained look tightened Caitlyn's face. "It turns out he had even more distasteful designs on Teresa. But don't worry, she played him for a fool and kept her honor intact. He let her use his ranch for her purposes, no questions asked."

"What purposes?" Benavides hooked his thumb toward the picture windows behind him. "She did all our work here."

"All the work on *our* plan," Caitlyn said. "She had another."

"What other plan? She never told me."

"She built a missile launcher to destroy the wormhole's equilibrator ring."

Benavides' eyebrows lowered. "Months ago you told her blowing up the wormhole's containment system would destroy Svoboda City. What the hell makes you think she didn't understand that?"

Another test of what the UN turncoat told the Benavides family? Stone stared glumly at the old man. Better guess right–

"I'm sure she knows what will happen," Caitlyn said. "I can only assume she's decided the benefit to Freeland is worth the cost."

"You better have more than an assumption. What's your proof?"

"Chalmers here. After he escaped from Teresa and the others, he doubled-back and reconnoitered Kovar's ranch. He shot video of Teresa moving the missile launcher off-site on one of your company's trucks. After I captured him, I extracted the video and validated it. It's real."

Benavides paled and seemed to shrink. He looked older than Stone had ever before seen him. "How can it be real? Teresa and I talked right after you told her what would happen if we blew up the wormhole's containment system. Killing tens of thousands of our fellow colonists was too high a price, no matter the gain. Better to blockade our end of the wormhole, and lynch Kovar and executive Schmied and the other traitors."

"Something changed her mind." Caitlyn's cheeks tightened. "I wish I knew what. Knowing would help me talk her out of destroying the equilibrator ring."

Some vigor returned to Benavides, lifting his chin and firming his eyes. "When you find Teresa, tell her I demand she not blow up the wormhole. We're not going to scorch our new earth to deny it to the UN hordes."

"I'll tell her that. Once I find her. I know you don't know where she is, but do you have any thought where she might be? Any lead you can offer would help me prevent the disaster she wants to unleash."

Benavides' eyes narrowed. His gaze flicked like a scanning radar between Caitlyn and Stone. "I might have something," he said after a time. "I'll tell you after you kill Chalmers."

CHAPTER 18

Stone's heart pounded like a gigantic gong. He turned his head to Caitlyn, taking in Benavides and the scrawny young men with his peripheral vision. The young men shifted their assault rifles closer to firing position, but neither one aimed at him. *You get the one behind our couch, I'll take care of Benavides and the other one.*

Caitlyn locked her hazel eyes on Benavides. "Sure. Tell me where."

"Right here will do fine."

"We'll get blood all over the sofa and the floor–"

"I can afford a few planks of synthwood," Benavides said. "Any blood that won't wash off the leather will give it character. Don't you think?" He peered at Caitlyn.

She shrugged. "Your choice, Lukas." Gaze still fixed on Benavides, a smile in her eyes, she reached to the small of her back. *Almost. You get the one behind us, I'll take the other two.*

Stone subvoked, *I'm a better shot–*

Caitlyn drew. The sleek black pistol swallowed light as she swept it up to aim at Benavides' chest.

Stone pulled out his snub-nosed revolver. Leaped and turned, cocking the revolver with the edge of his left hand. Caitlyn's pistol barked and his roared. Two more pistol shots echoed off the wooden walls and Stone fired again. The scrawny man tumbled backward, two ragged gouges in his chest pulsing with blood.

Stone pivoted. A glimpse of Benavides slumped in his chair, bleeding from a chest wound. The young man behind him lowered his assault rifle with shaking hands. Range so close even spray-and-pray would get them.

From behind the couch, a burst of automatic fire pounded Stone's ears.

Stone's arm shot out, fixed on target. He fired. Blood splattered from the young man's thin neck, gouted out as he collapsed nervelessly. His assault rifle slipped from his hands. Stone's ears rang so much from the gunfire the assault rifle seemed to silently hit the floor.

Back to the first scrawny young man. He lay on the floor behind the couch, empty eyes aimed at the bullet holes he'd put in the ceiling. His assault rifle straddled his open right hand.

A common enough sight. For Stone. *How are you?* Stone subvoked to Caitlyn.

His implantable blocked the nerve impulses trying to send the ringing sensation from his ears to his brain. Even so, Caitlyn's subvoked voice sounded small. *I'm... fine.... You?*

Unhurt. For now. Anyone within a quarter-mile heard the gunfire. We have to get out of here. Stone mashed his revolver's safety on and tucked it into the back of his waistband. He went around the couch on trembling legs.

He's still alive.

Stone lurched. He turned his tunneled vision on the scrawny young man's empty face. Near enough to dead if he wasn't already.

He's trying to tell me something.

Benavides, she meant. Stone looked over his shoulder. A flicker of life remained in Benavides' narrow brown eyes. Sweat shone on the old man's forehead. His lips moved and blood burbled from his mouth. Stone's implantable read Benavides' lips and overlaid subtitles on Stone's field of vision.

Blowing the wormhole would be worth the cost.

Blood gushed from Benavides' mouth. His back stiffened and his fingers clawed at his chair's tan leather arms. A wet, choking sound emerged from his throat, followed by silence.

"Time to go," Stone said. He reached with thick fingers for the dead boy's assault rifle.

Caitlyn squeezed shut her eyes, shook her head. She stood up and faced Stone. Then she opened her wide hazel eyes. "You're right." She followed Stone's path around the couch. "What are you doing?"

"I'm down to three rounds in the revolver. Not enough." He lifted the assault rifle, glanced at LED numbers on the bottom of the magazine. Fifteen rounds. His finger slipped over the selector, reengaged, switched the assault rifle to semiauto. "Grab the other one."

The room stank of propellant and blood. "I have two spare magazines for my pistol."

Stone snapped his head around and scowled at her. Movement visible through the picture windows behind her caught his attention. Two unarmed men stood on the other side of a synthwood fence, eyes wide. One pointed at the dead young man behind Benavides' chair.

"We go. Now!" Stone said.

With a sweep of her long blond hair, Caitlyn glanced over her shoulder. "Dammit. Car, start your engine. Stay locked until we arrive."

Stone and Caitlyn ran to the front door. Her green sedan waited on the gravel driveway, ten yards away. They sprinted down the path, Stone's head swiveling. A human shape, to the right. One of Benavides' men, in a triangular firing stance.

"Hey! Stop!" A bullet panged along the side of the green sedan and a gunshot roared.

Stone fired back, three wild shots on the run.

"Unlock and open!" Caitlyn shouted at her sedan. The doors on the near side popped open. Stone yanked one wide. The graze line of the bullet revealed gray alloy underneath the paint. Caitlyn slipped past him and onto the rear seat.

Stone glanced toward the shooter. Belly-down on grass near the corner of the house, the shooter grimaced under a shock of black hair, left hand clutching his thigh. No one else coming around the ranch house.

Yet. Stone climbed in and pulled the doors shut. Before his rump hit the front seat, he said, "Move, move!"

"Do it!" Caitlyn told the sedan. The tires flung clattering gravel, starting on a path to swing by the downed shooter and along the gravel driveway toward the side road.

Stone glanced over his shoulder. The shooter moved his pistol hand along the ground, fired, again, again.

Something slapped the right rear tire. "Warning," said the sedan in a smooth female voice. "Low tire pressure detected. I will reduce speed."

Caitlyn drew in a breath. "Do it."

The motor's low hum grew quieter and the car slowed. "Are you kidding?" Stone said. "We can go full speed a hundred miles on a flat tire. On the rim, even, if we needed to."

"But we might lose control–"

"Only if–" The car swung onto the main driveway, bound for the road. Behind Caitlyn, men ran after them, with glances behind as if a vehicle joined the chase. "–Benavides' men catch up and try forcing us off the road."

Caitlyn looked over her shoulder, then turned back to the cabin. "Full speed!"

The car accelerated downslope. The right rear wheel shook. "Destination?"

"The ITB motor pool in Svoboda City. We'll switch cars there," she said to Stone.

They still had to find Teresa and the missile launcher. But first things first. A red pickup came into view at the crest of the slope, next to the ranch house. Men climbed over the sides and tailgate. The red pickup accelerated, kicking up a dust cloud like a comet's tail.

Stone crouched on the carpet next to the left side doors. "Open the windows," he said.

Glass whirred down. Wind noise and the crunch of gravel from outside joined a rhythmic thump coming from the ruined tire. He slid the selector to full auto and raised the assault rifle to his shoulder. The sedan reached the cattle guard at the end of the driveway and pounded across the spaced pipes. Making the turn, the back end of the sedan slewed to the right. Gave him a straight shot at the red pickup.

He squeezed the trigger. Gunfire slammed his ears and hot casings spun to the cabin's carpeted floor.

The green sedan finished its turn and sped down the road toward Frichville Highway. Up the slope, glimpsed through a barbed wire fence along the road side, the red pickup stood at an angle, nose down, smoke seeping through the hood's seams.

"Lucky shot," Caitlyn said.

"I'll take it." Stone fell against the seat next to her, then checked the bottom of the magazine. The LEDs read *00*. He dropped the now-useless assault rifle on the floor.

"God willing our luck will hold to find Teresa."

Stone arched his eyebrow at her. The damaged wheel shook harder and sounded like metal sliced over gravel. "If we rely on luck, she'll beat us. Pull up all your intel so we can figure out where she might be."

Forty-five minutes later, they pulled out of the ITB motor pool in a blueberry-colored SUV. Tall, knobby tires lifted the SUV's sharp facets and the hatches of retractable accessories to pedestrian eye level.

From the forward-facing bench seat, Stone scowled at the flat surfaces angled slightly from one another making up the ceiling. "Anyone can see this vehicle is a recent Earth design."

"We've been together two hours and you're already tuning out when I talk to you?" Across the cabin, Caitlyn pointed the toe of her crossed leg toward him. Like Stone, she wore ITB-issue body armor from the neck down and a helmet sat on the seat next to her. "It's the only off-road vehicle we have available."

"Her lookouts will make us from two thousand yards."

"We have three hours to cover forty klicks between target sites. You'd rather walk?"

The SUV turned right, onto Blaha Boulevard in the direction of the wormhole. The knobby tires whispered on the pavement. Three hours, unless Teresa decided to destroy the equilibrator ring before Yadav and Deshmukh came through. Word that UN agents killed her grandfather and were hunting her now might change her mind....

He reached for the ITB-issue assault rifle lying on the seat to his right. A clean design of solid metal and a double magazine curved like a ram's horn. He checked the counter and the sights for the third time. Totally useless if Teresa destroyed the wormhole ahead of schedule. Would the gamma ray burst vaporize them instantly?

His implantable popped a notification window into his vision. *C. Fredriksen requests permission to project image and text.* "Let's review the first site," Caitlyn said.

"I was listening to that part." Stone dropped the assault rifle on the synthetic leather seat. "Your drone picked up a radar anomaly compatible with chaffed camo screens covering an area about twenty meters by forty, raised fourteen meters off the ground, at a location four klicks east-southeast of the wormhole—"

"You don't need to get pissy."

Stone opened his mouth to cut back. A pensive look in Caitlyn's hazel eyes stayed his tongue. She also worried that Teresa might destroy the wormhole early. Where he checked his equipment, she rehearsed her plan.

He sat up taller. *Approved*, he told his implantable. "I still might have missed something. A review is a good idea."

A relief map appeared in his vision, seeming to float at knee-height in the center of the cabin. A dirt road cut a tan, north-south gash across rolling fields of dark-green grasses. Scale two hundred yards per foot. Above one corner, a bobbing virtual compass pointed in the direction of the wormhole. Another corner held a floating countdown timer. ETA 9:04, 9:03....

Along the dirt road, at a site partially screened from the line of sight of ITB personnel at the wormhole by a low hill, a yellow fuzz of probability estimates swarmed like fog around a streetlight. Data picked up by Caitlyn's drones suggested what might be a mound of fill dirt—or a set of radar-boggling camouflage screens covering the missile launcher.

Caitlyn's toe swept through the edge of the map. She set both feet flat on the floor and leaned forward, elbows on knees. "Map LOS probabilities for this vehicle approaching the site by the dirt road. Both directions."

The map zoomed out, until three miles of countryside floated before them. A red circle surrounded the target site. Thick grayscale covered the tan line. The darkest shades of gray lurked at the map's edges and in dips in the rolling terrain. The gray generally lightened the nearer the red circle. To both north and south the last three hundred yards gleamed as white as Earth's full moon.

"We'll get well within two thousand yards before we're seen," Caitlyn said.

"Three hundred is the best case. At top speed, and assuming we want to stop when we get there, that's about ten seconds."

Caitlyn's gaze traced up and down the dirt road. "Maybe we don't stop. Drive by at high speed, see if there's anything suspicious, then go overland back at them."

Stone rolled his lips in and mashed them between his jaws. "If this is a false positive, your idea saves time."

"Sounds like you think this site is a false positive."

"It's in the gamma ray burst zone, isn't it?" He glanced at her. The narrow line of her nose pulled his gaze up to her hazel eyes.

A flicker in the map drew his attention back. Bright red covered the entire map, shaded slightly toward the south.

"There's your answer," Caitlyn said.

Indeed. A gamma ray burst from the wormhole would kill anyone within a mile of the site. "Assume they aren't suicidal. The other two target sites–" Each five kilometers from the wormhole, with one due north and the other south-south-west of it. "–are out of the main burst zone. Teresa deployed the missile launcher at one of those."

"That's a sensible, pragmatic assumption that would make perfect sense if we were sipping lattes on the Upper East Side."

Stone shook his head. "Nobody wants to die. No matter how much he says he would die for his cause."

"Says a man who believes in no cause at all."

Part of Stone bristled. A sensation like a steel blast door slammed shut behind his face. "Would I risk my life to save thousands of colonists if what you say is true?"

Well? asked the Jezhek persona. *Would you?*

Dammit, the cover stories techs at headquarters really botched this one.

Caitlyn angled her head. Blond locks trickled along her cheeks. "I shouldn't have said that. I applied my mental model of the type of men Gray operates onto you. But I don't know what kind of man you really are."

Stone's body armor itched between his shoulder blades. He squirmed his back against the seat. "Doesn't matter." He sat taller. "We have eight minutes till we reach the site. Time to map our approach–"

They talked through the plan before the SUV turned from the paved highway onto the dirt road. Visual observation while driving at full speed past the target site. If Teresa's men and equipment were present, they would dismount the SUV behind a low rise, then sprint a hundred and forty yards toward the target. No time for subtlety– Teresa would need only a few seconds to launch the missiles if she chose. Their body armor and helmets would reduce the odds of wounds or death.

"One thousand meters to target site," the SUV said to their auditory nerves.

Stone lifted his angular black helmet by the chin piece and opening for the raised visor. "Helmets on."

"Maximum safe speed," Caitlyn said to the SUV. She met Stone's gaze and nodded.

The SUV surged forward, bouncing and rattling on gravel and bare dirt. Stone and Caitlyn tugged their helmets down over their heads.

She pinched and swept her hand through air. The visibility overlay vanished from the map. A blue icon marked their vehicle racing down the dirt road. The map smoothly zoomed in, keeping their SUV near the northern edge and the target site in the center.

Zooming stopped. The SUV climbed out of the last hollow, about a quarter-mile from the target. Stone watched the view outside the window, right hand on the assault rifle, left hand on the chinpiece of his helmet. He'd pull the helmet off as soon as they called the site clear. Teresa wasn't fanatical enough to choose suicide.

The terrain levelled off. The SUV sped up, sent teeth-chattering vibration into the cabin. A hundred yards from the target, two seconds, one–

By the speeding SUV flashed a camo screen wall and two armed guards in dust-colored fatigues.

CHAPTER 19

Mouth suddenly dry, Stone snapped the visor over his eyes. Diagnostics flashed green and alphanumerics popped up in the visor's corners.

"Five seconds," Caitlyn said. A countdown timer added itself to the visual data filling Stone's vision.

The SUV followed a slight curve in the road. The ground rose on the right, blocking the lower half of the deployed camo screens from view. Brakes slammed. Rubber scraped over gravel. The rear wheels slipped and the antilock brakes pulsed like a heart under cardiac arrest.

Motion ceased and the right-side doors popped open. Caitlyn kicked wide the front door, Stone did the same to rear. In front of them, on the other side of the grass-tufted rise, chaff strips woven into the camo screens glittered in the afternoon sun.

Their feet hit the ground at the same time. Stone leaped over a roadside drainage ditch, Caitlyn right behind him.

Uphill they ran. Local grasses passed in a blur, glimpsed in passing as Stone's gaze roved the ground for mines and trip wires. Ground clear to the naked eye. Same to the sensors in his helmet, body armor, and assault rifle, as well as those emerged from hatches in the SUV.

"They didn't prepare well," Caitlyn said around huffing breaths.

"Or they've laid a trap."

Stone reached the top of the rise first. The camo screens stood and hung in front of him, angled and disjointed like the walls and roofs of some billionaire's mansion. Sixty yards to the nearest of the gigantic screens. At ground level, three boulders rose about a yard from the rocky ground, one at each corner of the site and the third midway between the others. Figures crouched, one at each boulder. Muzzles flashed. Small arms fire ripped the air. Bullets smacked the ground near Stone and whizzed by his helmeted head. His implantable filled his visor with the red traces of bullet trajectories.

"I've got the one on the right." Still running, Stone squeezed the trigger. His assault rifle vibrated against his hands. The helmet deployed internal mufflers and still his rifle roared in his ears. His rounds pinged off the right-most boulder and punched through the camo screen rising behind it. Behind him to his left, Caitlyn's assault rifle added to the din.

The men opposing them kept firing. Something punched Stone's left thigh, then his chest. Bullets stopped by his body armor. He ran, continued to fire. His implantable popped into his vision a blocky black line at ground level, across his path. Red and orange warning triangles bloomed across the bottom of his visor. Short-range motion sensor. Buried explosives. Jump and tuck–

The ground erupted under him. Shrapnel and pebbles rattled against his armored shins and uppers of his boots. Stone straightened his legs and hit the ground running. He swung the assault rifle up and fired at the man behind the boulder to the right.

His target lifted the rifle above his head and the top of the boulder. Fired without aiming. Lowered the rifle. Ran away in a crouch toward a gap between camo screens.

Still running, half his attention looking for more buried explosives, Stone fired at the retreating man. Rounds sprayed, tearing the camo screen and skipping off bare dirt between the site and the road. His visor counted his loaded magazine down to zero rounds. Stone ejected the empty and yanked a fresh magazine off hook-and-loop fabric at his waist.

Caitlyn fired. A single burst answered her. A glance to the left showed the far boulder unoccupied. Behind the middle boulder, the defender showed his back as he slipped under a raised flap in the camo screen.

Stone slammed the fresh magazine into his assault rifle. The camo screen concealed the last defender. Dammit. Stone held his fire and kept running.

"Going in. Right corner."

"Confirmed," Caitlyn replied. "I'm heading left."

Stone ran faster, looping outward on a trajectory to round the boulder. The camo screens facing the road came into view. He raised his assault rifle. No guards. Camo screens like tied-back curtains, giving an opening ten feet wide and tall. The hell? Too small and on the wrong side to launch missiles–

A pickup raced out of the dark interior. Two men in the cabin, three in the bed, all armed. Stone fired, The man on the near side of the pickup's bed toppled backward and out of sight. The pickup's rear wheels slewed across dirt and gravel. A glimpse of eyes stark in a boyish, blood-spattered face, kneeling toward his wounded buddy.

From inside the site, a second pickup sped out. Five men again. The one at the pickup's tailgate held a grenade launcher instead of a rifle.

Still running, Stone fired. One of his rounds punched the fender. Men fired back while the grenade carrier aimed at the opening. Fired.

The grenade arced into the opening. A muffled crump came from the grenade's detonation. Orange light glowed in the dark interior.

A moment later, flames licked at the bottom edges of the camo screens.

Stone's feet slowed and his breaths rasped inside the helmet. In his mind, all the pieces fell into place. Dammit. "Stay out. Monitor the road on the off chance they come back."

No reply. Flames crawled up the edges of the opening.

"Head in the game, keyhole kop!"

Her thick inhalation came over the radio. "Why didn't they launch missiles at the wormhole?"

"Because the missile launcher isn't here!" Flames worked along the bottom of the camo screen, coming toward the gap through which the defender had retreated seconds earlier. "Going in to confirm." He ran to the gap. The approaching flames warmed his right arm. Bitter smoke seeped between his helmet and visor. A vent fan whined in his ear like an insect. Stone dropped to hands and feet, assault rifle rigid between his glove and the rocky ground. He bear-crawled through the gap. Winced at heat and smoke as he stood. *Record video*, he told his implantable. *Relay to Caitlyn.*

Save for tufted grasses and dirt creased by the tire tracks of the two pickups, the space walled and roofed by the camo screens was empty. His voice snarled. "You seeing this?"

"I've seen enough," she said over the radio. Stone spun around, faced the gap. She added, "Get out of there."

Half the camo screen flanking the opening now burned. Flames reached the top and tongued at one of the roof screens. More flames danced at the edge of the gap. Only a second before the next camo screen would catch fire.

Stone sprinted and dove through the gap like a receiver stretching the ball for the first down marker. Flame baked him like the thick hands of hell's defensive lineman. High temp sensors squawked inside his helmet and orange-red halos ringed the lower legs of a man-shaped icon in the middle of his vision. Pain raced over his shins and calves. At what temp would ITB body armor melt?

He rolled on his side, pounded his lower legs against the ground. Caitlyn kicked dirt at his legs.

The squawks faded from his helmet and the icon vanished. Pain throbbed in his lower legs. Stone winced and sat upright. He flipped up the visor to get a better look. Ripples marred the body armor over his shins.

Caitlyn lifted her visor and crouched beside his lower legs. "How badly are you hurt?" she asked over the crackle of the burning camo screens.

"I'll manage." He set his palms on the dusty ground and pushed himself to his feet. Body armor scraped over scorched skin. Through gritted teeth he said, "Dammit."

"You're sure you'll manage?"

He sucked a breath through his teeth, looked up. Flames engulfed the camo screens roofing the site, higher than Freeland's sun hanging halfway down the western sky. He subvoked to his implantable, received an exact ETA close to what he'd guessed. 1:46:16 before Yadav and Deshmukh would traverse the wormhole.

Bitter smoke made Stone clear his throat. He squinted against the heat of the burning camo screens, shielded his eyes against the local sun. "I have to."

Ten minutes later, Caitlyn said, "They're heading to the site south of the wormhole."

In the middle of the cabin, a live feed from her drone showed the two pickups a mile and a half from the wormhole, turning left off the highway, heading southwest.

On the SUV's rear seat, helmet and assault rifle flanking him, Stone leaned forward. Cool air from the vents chilled the sweat clinging to his hair and nape. A burn gel numbed his bared shins. He swallowed cold water, capped the bottle, and dropped it on the seat beside him. "Meaning the missile launcher is at the northern one."

Caitlyn eyed the turning pickups. "Teresa knows we're still looking for her. She'd want ten–nine extra personnel to strengthen her defenses against us."

"She may believe the missile launcher is still hidden. She would expect aerial recon to track those two pickups all the way to their desti-nation. She's talented enough to reuse them as decoys." He checked the countdown. 1:35:13. "Especially because we only have time for one more bite at the apple."

Caitlyn drew in a long breath through her narrow nose. She watched the map as if some answer would emerge from it. The view panned and blurred a moment before refocussing.

The corners of Stone's mouth lifted. "Unless we split up."

Across the cabin, Caitlyn's smooth brow creased. "I don't think that will work. It will take thirty minutes for another car to drive here from base. And then half as many of us would be going up against more of her men, who'd defend the target at all costs."

Stone's grin widened. "Who said anything about a car?"

Her hazel eyes skewered him. "How the hell else can you get there?"

Smirk still on his face, he shrugged. "Depends on the specs of your drone."

CHAPTER 20

Under a few high, puffy clouds, Freeland's sun hung low in the western sky. Long shadows of cattle and ranching robots flowed over the khaki and green-black contours of the rolling plain a mile below Stone.

He hung spreadeagled beneath the eight-foot-long quadrotor drone. Four handcuffs, each with one bracelet around a dull blue, nanotube alloy rotor arm, held Stone by his wrists and ankles. If he twisted his head left or right he could see dabs of pale red moldable explosive on the handcuff chains, and minuscule cylinders of gray steel, the detonators, jutting out of the explosive putty. The detonators' ready lights slowly blinked green.

His stomach clenched, accustomed to free fall or descent under an open parachute, but not dangling under a drone. The downdraft from the unshielded rotors howled around him, buzzed in his ears and sent painful vibrations through the drone's frame against his back. Though gauntlets and greaves of body armor protected his skin, the handcuffs set his hands and feet to tingling. If even one of the four detonators failed when the time came, he could be dangling with one free hand with dozens of Teresa's henchmen surrounding him, weapons drawn and firing.

Stone's laugh filled his helmet. The action he lived for, just moments away. All he needed was to descend to the target site.

His implantable projected a red circle onto the mottled ground, slightly ahead and to his left. A dirt track ran to the circle from Kovar Road a mile and a half to the east. The red circle ringed a feature on the northern face of a hill. The feature cast a shadow as if it were a rounded outcrop of rock.

It could well be. No way to tell from this height.

Time to descend.

He subvoked instructions to the drone. The buzz and vibration of the rotors faded to a fraction of their former intensity. His internal organs floated inside his abdominal cavity, and for a fleeting moment his gorge rose.

Free fall. Every few seconds, rotors would spin up for a moment to keep him on target. The wind roared now, shrieking past him, slapping the assault rifle mounted by hook-and-loop fabric against his chest. The assault rifle stayed in place, though, along with three incendiaries from the cargo bin of Caitlyn's SUV. The red circle grew larger, and what might be a seam between camo screens resolved itself.

So too did a rectangular object positioned with its long axis across the dirt track about fifty yards from the target. The object's tan color lightened at one end. The lighter end cast a longer shadow than the rest of the object.

Realization flooded him. A pickup blocked the dirt track. And behind it, four shapes barely bigger than pinpoints: Teresa's henchmen.

The ground rushed toward him. He made out four more pickups parked between the blocker and the site. The camo screens roofing the site resolved into discrete shapes and discernible angles. The red circle projected onto his vision narrowed. A few subvoked commands focused the red circle off-center on the site's northern side, where lines and shadows indicated a pole held up a large camo screen.

The altimeter display in his visor dropped into triple digits. From over nine hundred feet to over eight hundred in an eyeblink. Close enough to make out visible splotches of paint, woven streaks of anti-radar chaff. One last inhalation. A heartbeat like a pounding drum.

The drone's rotors roared. Five gees of deceleration yanked Stone's wrists and ankles behind his body like a medieval torture device. The body armor shielding his abdomen smashed onto the camo screen tented by the hidden pole. He swayed and the roaring rotors stuttered, returning him to level. The camo screen billowed downward, exposing part of the interior as Stone hovered.

The missile launcher's tubes peeked over the far end of the red shipping container. Thick data cables snaked over the shipping container's end wall, plugged into ports in the missile launcher's gray plastic base.

Right hand, he subvoked.

The red moldable at his right wrist detonated. Heat singed the hairs on the back of his hand and on his lower arm. He reached for the first incendiary. Pulled it free of the burry fabric on his chest and armed the contact fuse with a single motion. Threw the incendiary at the data cable ports on the missile launcher's base.

An explosion rattled off the shipping container's steel walls. Flame gouted up as he threw the second incendiary. Another explosion. He threw the third.

Descent plan.

The drone dropped below the top of the shipping container. The altimeter showed single digits. Two more detonations and his legs fell free. He dangled by his left hand, all the muscles of his arm clenched. His feet touched dirt and the fourth dab of red moldable detonated.

Stone spun around, facing north, where the fallen camo screen covered the other end of the data cables and three or four human-sized shapes wrestling under the fabric.

Cover my back, he subvoked through his implantable to the drone. The buzz of the drone's motors drifted away from him, ready to charge at hostiles and spin up its unshielded rotors to thousands of rpm.

He pulled the assault rifle off his chest, racked the slide, thumbed the safety off. He fired a three-shot burst into the nearest of the figures struggling under the camo screen, then another. Aimed at the next figure, fired two more bursts. Repeat. Within two seconds, he ejected the empty magazine. The camo screen shrouded the four human-sized shapes, now barely moving.

Stone slotted in the next magazine when a bullet punched him in the right thigh.

Despite the flames licking over the top of the shipping container and the sweat trickling down his cheeks, he turned coolly. A line of three young men, clad in flannel and denim, fabbed plastic rifles in their hands. The first two gaped at the fallen camo screen, the burning missile launcher. Only the third aimed at Stone. A rifle bullet cracked the air, slammed Stone's forehead.

Stone reeled a moment. Panic flooded his mouth–two inches lower and the bullet could have pierced the visor–but he kept it down. A burst from his assault rifle tore open the rifleman's chest. The young man tumbled to the dirt. Blood gushed from his wounds.

Stone swung the muzzle toward the next man in line. He died, eyes still starkly full of whites.

The third showed only a glimpse of his back as he slipped through a gap between camo screens walling the site.

The air under the remaining camo screens stunk of burning plastic and scorched metal. Stone went forward past the side of the shipping container. Glanced right. Three of Teresa's henchmen ran between camo screens while a fourth raised his rifle with both hands. The drone's rotor slashed at the plastic. A plastic shred whipped at a rotor. The drone bucked but stayed airborne. The man dropped his rifle, tripped as he turned, scrambled on hands and knees for the passageway between camo screens.

Stone aimed, but took his finger off the trigger. Not the high-value target he sought. He glanced left. A shadowy shape behind the camo screens forming the site's northern wall moved frantically to the east.

He swung the assault rifle toward the shadowy figure. Fired a burst. Missed.

Over the roar of fire inside the shipping container and the muffling of camo screens came a voice from outside, to the east, melodious and unexpectedly cool. "Plan B! Runaway Scrape!"

Teresa.

Stone's head pounded. Runaway Scrape? The Jezhek persona welled up in the back of Stone's mind, Texians fleeing Santa Ana while Sam Houston prepared for battle.

Stone glanced at the eastern exits her henchmen had just taken. Unlikely they would cover them, but if they did, and fired one lucky shot.... He trotted north, trampling the fallen, billowing camo screen. He stepped over an unmoving human-sized shape. Blood squelched under his boot. He sidestepped through a gap between hanging screens, swung up his muzzle.

Nothing but tufts of sprangletop casting long shadows across a slope. Behind the corner of the camo screens, vehicle doors slammed. He crouched and loped forward. Gravel rattled under tires.

Stone peeked around the corner as the second pickup drove off. Men crowded the bed, plastic rifles pointed at the sky. With a thirty yard head start, the first pickup veered off the track to loop around the blocking truck. Through the rear window and a rising cloud of dust, Stone glimpsed a sheaf of Teresa's shoulder-length blond hair.

He dropped prone and raised his assault rifle. Easy range, one burst–

Bullets spangled the ground around him. A third pickup, crowded with men peering over the tailgate with horizontal rifles. The third pickup flung pebbles from its tires and started down the track.

Stone slithered back behind the corner of the camo screens. More fire from the third pickup kicked up dust in front of him. He tracked the third pickup's progress down the track by its dust cloud.

He crept forward. The blocking pickup slewed its back end toward him, then followed the other three away. His gaze darted around, hunting motion, finding none. He peered at the cab and wheels of the fourth pickup. No one lurked either place.

Stone stood then and blew out a breath. Ahead, the pickups carrying Teresa and her henchmen disappeared behind a high contour. Flames crackled behind him, punctuated by a sharp snap and a billowing sound. He glanced over his shoulder. All the camo screens roofing the site had collapsed. Flame filled the smothered outline of the shipping container and trickled along the fallen camo screens like lava.

He'd accomplished his primary mission. Yadav and Deshmukh would traverse the wormhole unaware how close they'd come to destruction. Teresa and her henchmen could go to ground, but not forever. Between American soldiers compelled into peacekeeping and the poorly-trained but numerous forces the resettled population could field, she and her remaining personnel would be trapped. Not Stone's mission... but the dust clouds of Teresa's caravan remained in view.

A grin split his face. Don't worry, Teresa. We're just getting started.

He trotted to the fourth pickup. *Call Caitlyn.*

She came online a moment later. "Did you find them?"

Yes. The drone insertion worked flawlessly. I destroyed the missile launcher and neutralized six hostiles before they could react.

The sound of her released breath filled his helmet. "Good. That's good. I passed the other site a moment ago. Totally empty. Glad you guessed right. If we hadn't split up–"

After action reports later. Teresa and about fifteen to twenty of her personnel are in retreat. Four pickups heading toward Kovar Road. I'll send the drone up to track them. I'm going to follow.

"How? I can't handcuff you back to the drone's rotor arms."

She left a pickup behind. Do you have a script to hack into vehicles built on Freeland?

"Do you need to unlock doors or start motors?"

His boots scuffed to a halt next to the fourth pickup's cab. He reached for the door handle and tugged. *Both.*

"On its way." A progress bar bisected the pickup's dirt-smudged window and rapidly filled with green. A bright chime rang inside his helmet.

Do it, he told his implantable. The script popped up a window into the lower left corner of his vision. Alphanumeric combinations cycled by, too rapidly to read.

By way of his implantable, he ordered the drone up and after the caravan of four pickups. He followed the drone's flight to the east until its blue underbelly faded against the sky. Faint residues of the dust clouds from Teresa's caravan remained above the rolling terrain.

The window flashed green. Another bright chime. The pickup's door opened slightly.

Stone tugged the handle, flung the door wide. Climbed in as green telltales lit up the instrument panel and the motor hummed to life. His left hand rested on the wheel, his right on the shift lever mounted on the steering column.

Full manual, he relayed through his implantable. Limbs jerky from adrenaline hangover, he pulled down the shift lever and mashed the accelerator. The rear wheels skidded, then griped the gravel track. He raced up and down the terrain's contours. Dusty land dotted with dark-green slipped by, barely seen in the corners of his eye.

Ahead, a westerly wind thinned the dust cloud over Kovar Road. Teresa's caravan had made the turn onto asphalt.

But which direction? *What does the drone show?*

A green line sprung into view above the track ahead. Bent in the middle, it pointed an arrowhead to the right.

Stone crested a roll in the terrain. His pickup's shadow, edges jagged by gravel and sparse grass, ran downslope toward a stop sign and an intersecting strip of mottled gray pavement. He eased the wheel to the left, then without stopping turned hard right and stomped the accelerator as he hit the apex of the turn. Tires squealed once on the asphalt, then whispered as the pickup surged ahead.

Range?

Red alphanumerics appeared in the center bottom of the windshield: *804 m -21 m/s.* He might close the gap before Teresa could reach the main highway between Svoboda City and the wormhole.

Stone jammed the pedal even harder against the floor. With his gaze on the road and his hands on the wheel, he rode calmly in the eye while a hurricane of speed and impending violence whirled around him.

Over the top of a swell in the ground. A shallow dishing in the terrain gave an unimpeded view of the intersection with the main highway six hundred yards ahead. Teresa's four pickups approached the intersection. Brake lights bloomed like distant bloody flowers. The first pickup rolled through the stop sign, turning left toward Svoboda City and speeding up. Perhaps only in his imagination, for a moment blond hair framed by the pickup's rear window seemed to catch the setting sun.

He raised his rump off the seat, put more weight on his right foot. The speedometer needle didn't budge. Dammit.

The next pickup turned. The next. Still four hundred yards–at this range, a left-handed shot out his window would merely waste ammunition. The last pickup turned left.

He took a breath. Take the turn at high speed and he'd close with them on the main highway–

Over the whisper of tires and the hum of the motor came a siren. From the west. From the wormhole.

"Where are you?" came Caitlyn's voice.

Kovar Road. A quarter mile from the main highway. You?

"A mile west of you." The sirens sounded louder now. "I'm waiting for Yadav and Deshmukh's motorcades to pass."

Motorcades?

Red warning icons popped up on his vision. ITB priority one. Civilian traffic barred from motorcade path. At the intersection, the siren wailed, louder, its source motionless. A motorcycle cop with a fluorescent green ITB vest pulled tight over his paunch balanced himself and his bike on his left foot. His motorcycle straddled the center line of Kovar Road, rear wheel on the thick white intersection stripe in Stone's lane.

The motorcycle cop looked up. Through his helmet's eyehole, wide, panicked eyes showed against pink skin.

Stone slammed the brakes. His tires chuffed on the pavement. The front grill stopped ten feet from the motorcycle cop.

The cop's eyes narrowed to a glare. He stiffly swung his right leg over the motorcycle, then waddled around to face Stone with crossed arms.

Stone barely noticed. Behind the motorcycle, the first car of Yadav and Deshmukh's motorcade cruised toward Svoboda City.

CHAPTER 21

As the shadows lengthened, the motorcade's stretch sedans drove by. All identical, black carbon fiber facets pushed out by half-inch-thick slabs of alloy armor. No way to tell which held security guards and which held heads of governments. The motorcade's sedate pace kept the Ashoka wheel and swastika flags of Hindurashtra and the Ganges Republic limp on the sedan's front corners. The taillights of the sedans and the spinning red-and-blue of the motorcycle cop's gumball machine grew brighter as Freeland's sun plunged below the horizon.

After the twelfth vehicle passed, the next one took a moment longer to draw even with Stone. A blue-and-white SUV with an ITB logo on its side. For long seconds, the spinning lights on its roof tinged the dashboard of Stone's pickup red, then blue. Finally, the SUV drove on.

Stone touched the brake pedal. Shifted into drive. Looked up.

The motorcycle cop slowly shook his head. His gaze fixed on Stone's throughout the gesture and held firm even after his head stopped moving. He uncrossed his arms then and with deliberation remounted his bike. A slow scan of the motorcycle's instrument panel made the heel of Stone's hand rise toward the horn. Stone sucked in a breath and drew his hand back.

One final glare from the cop, then he weaved his motorcycle into line at the back of the motorcade.

Stone rolled the last feet toward the intersection. The pickup's sensors and his peripheral vision picked up motion from his right. Dammit, not more delay–

A chunky shape, purplish-blue, followed the motorcade. An SUV, recently fabbed on Earth. On the rear seat he glimpsed sandy blond hair.

After you, he said, as Caitlyn drove by.

"You couldn't beat the motorcade?"

A traffic cop blocked off the intersection. One of yours, which took running him over off the table. Stone turned left onto the main highway and accelerated.

"You're really learning how to collaborate with us."

Stone eased off the accelerator, held formation three car-lengths behind Caitlyn. The highway descended into a shallow depression. Fully shadowed now. The taillights of the motorcade glowed like red binary stars. The blue-black sky ahead at the eastern horizon looked like a bruise spreading out and up. *No flirting until we take her into custody.*

He blinked once, both at his tone and what it told him. Did he really lack the urge to bed Caitlyn? A subtle nod. Yes, really. He'd seduced enough women that one more, no matter how blond her hair or hazel her eyes, meant nothing. More, he didn't care if Caitlyn sensed his thoughts from the way he spoke.

Her voice tiptoed past his tone. "Don't worry. The drone is tracking Teresa and her remaining cadre."

I'm sure it is. But I trust my own eyes more.

"They're travelling eastbound at ninety miles an hour, about six miles from Svoboda City. Wait a second."

Stone subvoked commands to his wearable. Video feed from the drone popped up over the pickup's nav screen. Her next words oriented him to the video. "They're slowing. Looks like they'll turn right. Yes."

Destination?

"I can't tell," she said. "Drone camera, zoom out. Implantable, meld video feed with stored map and overlay positions of interest."

As they crept along behind the motorcade, Stone gave long glances to the drone's zoomed-out, augmented video feed. A scale marker in the lower left corner showed the screen held a rectangle about twelve miles by ten, splotched by the long and growing shadows of rolling terrain. The wormhole highway ran into Svoboda City along one of the short sides, where it formed roughly a right angle with the Novy Morava River. Bright, meandering lines highlighted the road network. Dozens of red dots marked houses, barns, and bioseeding facilities. The intensities of the red dots varied with the likelihood Teresa's four pickups could hide under a roof.

Stone glanced again at the map again, held the image in his mind's eye as he drove. Ten sites maxed out the intensity scale. Teresa might be leading her caravan to any one of them.

"What's the chance she'll make a stand?" Caitlyn asked.

Years of experience helped Stone half-consciously weigh possibilities. *Slim. If we fix her position, we could call a rapid response force through the wormhole before she could rally enough of her allies to break our observation.*

"How would she expect that?"

The UN turncoat might have told her about our capabilities. Unarticulated thoughts slipped solidly into place. *She's going to deploy decoys. Her four pickups plus other vehicles she's stashed out there, separating and slipping away under cover of darkness.*

Fifty feet ahead, Caitlyn's SUV crested a rise. The setting sun spotlighted a nod of her head. "That's the best read on the sitch, I think."

A smirk crept into his voice. *You don't think. You know.*

They rode in silence toward the indigo eastern horizon for the next five minutes. The taillights of Yadav and Deshmukh's motorcade flowed ahead of them like a sluggish river. On the augmented map, Teresa's caravan showed as four radar reflections, winding southeastward toward the river. Some red dots faded and others engorged themselves on the map as Caitlyn's implantable recalculated probabilities based on Teresa's line of travel.

A plan formed in Stone's mind.

Six miles from Svoboda City, the motorcade passed an intersecting paved road and proceeded around a curve. Caitlyn's SUV turned right onto the paved road. Stone followed, thoughts running ahead to Teresa's caravan.

Three motionless bands of bright red LED hovered in the deepening twilight.

He mashed the brake pedal. *Why the hell are you stopping?*

The left-hand doors of the SUV opened. Caitlyn leaned out, blond hair and hazel eyes stark in contrast to the black body armor ending at her neck. She waved him toward the SUV. "This vehicle is hardened against roadside bombs. Is yours?"

He chuckled out a breath. *Good point. Before I join you, I'll check if this pickup's nav has one of the target locations as a preset. If it does, we'll follow it right to her.*

Caitlyn frowned. The pickup's headlights washed out crinkles in her brow. "You expect that to work?"

Stone pressed the button to open the window. "No. Teresa's talented at the craft. But her subordinates might have gotten sloppy." He pressed softbuttons on the nav screen, quickly figured out the menus. There. Locations in memory. His finger jabbed the button. Benavides Ranch. Kovar Ranch. Kovar Construction's office. Diners and bars in Svoboda City. He swiped, scrolling downward.

His wearable popped up text. *No matches with any location identified by Caitlyn.*

Worth a shot, but still, damn. Stone shoved open the driver's door and clomped his armored boots to the asphalt. He retrieved the assault rifle from the seat, then walked to the purplish-blue SUV. "Not sloppy enough."

"That doesn't matter anymore," Caitlyn said from the rear of the SUV's dark interior. "She stopped."

Stone climbed in and pulled the door shut behind him. He slipped onto the seat next to her. *Update me as we go.*

Headlights off, the SUV pulled smoothly away. The ribbon of pavement, a darker slice across the shadowed landscape, whispered under the tires. Inside the cabin, projected in the air in the middle of the cabin, a rectangular structure of sheet metal and concrete block filled the drone's camera view with the amalgamated true and false colors of video, radar, and infrared data.

"A bioseeding facility, unused for about twenty years but still listed as active by the local government. We believe it's a single open interior, about thirty meters by fifty." The view rotated in front of Stone. "Three garage doors face the road. Four personnel doors, one on each side. High windows around the perimeter, just under the roofline."

"Location?"

"Surrounded by ranchland nine miles from here. A mile from the river, five miles south of Svoboda City."

Stone's gaze swung up to the nightscape sliding past. His mouth tightened. "Our speed?"

"Ninety-five."

He spun his stare to her. "Five and a half minutes. If she has decoys stashed there, she'll scatter before we arrive."

Caitlyn folded her arms and pointed the knee of her crossed left leg at him. "The SUV is implementing our standard protocol for safe high-speed travel, based on road conditions, traffic, and ambient light."

Stone unclenched his fists. He stalked across the cabin, sat on the left side of the front seat. Twisted at the waist, his hands pawed across the headrest and the upholstered shelf behind it. "Pop out the manual controls."

"It doesn't have any."

She had to be kidding him. Stone opened his mouth. Words eluded him. He untwisted and sagged onto the seat, and his gaze landed on the bioseeding facility slowly rotating in his view. "Five minutes gives her more than enough time to deploy her decoys."

"Maybe she doesn't have any."

In the display, all three garage doors rolled up. A dozen vehicles raced out of the facility, four through each open door. One group of four headed south, toward a small town with a vehicle ferry across the river. The other eight drove north, toward Svoboda City.

Stone bit back an insult. After the delay caused by Yadav and Deshmukh's motorcade, even he couldn't have driven quickly enough to the bioseeding facility. He let his eyes fall closed and slowly breathed in.

Caitlyn's voice sounded small. "That was a silly hope."

He opened his eyes. "Don't beat yourself up. At least not now. Focus on figuring out which group to follow."

The eight northbound vehicles slowed for an intersection. The first four turned left, angling away from Stone and Caitlyn's route in the general direction of the wormhole. The last four turned to the right, onto a path soon intersecting a riverfront road that three miles further north became Novy Morava Avenue in Svoboda City.

"Our odds just got worse," Caitlyn said.

Stone's voice sliced through the cabin. "Not if we can outthink her."

The drone's camera zoomed out to show all three of Teresa's caravans. Doubts oozed inside Stone. The shortest path across the river, to the weapons stockpiles and manpower reserve at the Benavides ranch, ran through Svoboda City. Teresa would know it, and would infer that he knew it. Had she sent decoys on the shortest route, expecting him to intercept? Or did she expect him to conclude the four vehicles heading directly to Svoboda City were decoys and she traveled by another group, and thus she took the shortest route? Or...?

A hunch slid into his mind. The corners of his mouth parted in a lazy grin. "Which we just did."

CHAPTER 22

The SUV slowed and popped open its left-hand doors. The damp, fertile smell of the river, barely visible in starlight thirty yards away, wafted into the SUV's cabin.

Stone eased the doors wide and jumped out, landing in a jog on smooth asphalt. Footsteps thudded behind him. A glance over his shoulder showed Caitlyn kept pace, her black body armor swallowing starlight. She nodded once and her hazel eyes seemed incongruous behind her visor.

Doors dangling, the SUV accelerated away, its whispering engine barely echoed by a low ridge running parallel to the road on the right. Stone followed a green arrow projected onto his optic nerves to the left, off the road, toward a grove of live oaks overlooking the river. The green arrow turned further to the left and pointed down.

He trotted into a position between two trees and dropped to his belly, facing back the direction they'd driven with his assault rifle in his hands. Undergrowth brushed his face. A rustle came from the other side of the tree to his right. *Ready,* she subvoked.

Stone studied the riverbank. There. Twenty-five yards away. Tied at one corner to a blackgum tree at the water's edge, a rubber sheet dimpled by rocks concealed three or four canoes. *See them?*

How many supply caches and vehicles has she hidden around this planet?

Not enough. Stone's lupine grin carried into his subvoked voice. *Can you accurately throw incendiaries that far?*

I'll manage.

Even if she couldn't, the explosions and bursting flame from her incendiaries, combined with his fire, should be enough to overwhelm Teresa and her men.

Stone called up the visual and infrared feeds from the drone a mile overhead. Thin flexible objects wavered in the starlight. Human body heat flickered around the edges. Teresa's force moved in groups of three or four, with two men holding up an infrared-reflective sheet over the rest of the group. On the other side of the low ridge, less than a quarter of a mile away and hiking briskly over a rancher's field. ETA three minutes. No sign they'd heard the SUV drive by.

Impending action pounded inside Stone like the slow beat of a bass drum. He pulled a ruggedized portable loudspeaker, a black cube about three inches on a side, from the hook-and-loop fabric on his chest. The hard rubber padding the edges barely yielded to his grip. He synced it to his implantable. Stood and threw it into bushes forty yards away, on the other side of the hidden canoes.

He went prone again and watched the top of the low ridge. Right on schedule, Teresa's force came over the crest. The first man held an infrared reflector sheet over his head. A breeze rippled the sheet as he started down toward a barbed-wire fence alongside the road.

Caitlyn drew in a breath. Grass rustled, sign she shifted her body.

Nerves. She knew how to kill, but not well. *Hold your throw until they're through the fence and across the road.*

I've got fire discipline. There's a rock under my hip, is all. A moment later, she said, *They're crossing the fence.*

The man in the lead rested his end of the infrared reflector on a fence post, then bent and pushed down a strand of wire. He slipped through the widened gap. Grabbed the end of the reflector and stood. Two figures slipped between wires, then the man at the other end of the reflector came through.

In the starshadow cast by the next group's reflector, Stone identified Teresa's lean, curvy figure. Wistful regret floated up from the

Jezhek persona for a moment, until his will abraded the sentiment away.

Moments later, the last of her men made it through. Her hard whisper carried to Stone under the live oaks. "The blackgum tree," Teresa said. "Rig the reflector sheets over the boats. Go!"

The column of men crossed the paved road toward the covered canoes. Stone's gaze cycled over the column. The lead man came within five yards of the blackgum. The thud of boots on pavement faded as the rear man reached the grass between the road and the river.

Now.

His assault rifle barked at the rear man, then his teammate holding the front end of the last reflector sheet. The men crumpled and the reflector sheet drifted onto the heads of two other men.

Firing sounds through the speaker, he subvoked. Bursts from an assault rifle roared from the distant bushes.

An explosion thundered short of the blackgum tree. Flame clung to the screaming figure of the column's lead man. He toppled and writhed on the ground.

Stone ejected an empty magazine, slotted a fresh one. Fired at the men holding the next-to-last reflector in the column.

Flip the speaker.

Across the distance and the sounds of the firefight, Stone couldn't hear the puff of compressed air. The speaker's next burst of firing sounds came from a slightly different position.

From riverbank to road, Teresa's men shouted and groaned. Arms pointed toward the bushes near the ruggedized speaker. At the front of the column, men slipped out from under the infrared reflector and beat at the flames scorching the lead man.

The air under the live oaks stank of propellant and hot brass.

Caitlyn threw another incendiary. It rolled under the rubber sheet and detonated. Flames gobbled the grounded end of a canoe and spired toward the blackgum's branches.

Her next throw landed on the sheet. The explosive flash strobed like lightning. For an instant, Teresa and her men, both whole and wounded, appeared like statues in the open ground.

Flip again, Stone said. He fired a burst over the head of a man near Teresa. Enough time for the speaker to settle. *Relay and disguise my voice. More masculine and commanding.*

A green dot appeared in a corner of his vision. Relay ready.

Stone subvoked. On the other side of Teresa's column, a deep, gruff voice parroted his words. "Your escape is cut off! You're caught in our crossfire! Surrender now!"

The flames spreading over the sheet cast a red glow on men's hunching shoulders. Wide eyes darted in every direction.

Teresa's voice remained melodious despite the crackling flames and the agonized groans of her wounded. "No! We die for our planet!"

"Surrender now! You will receive fair trials. Reflectors down! Weapons down! Hands up!"

The huddled men gaped with slack jaws.

Teresa's voice gusted like a blizzard gale. "I have more balls than the goddam lot of you put together!"

"Surrender now!" Stone shouted through the speaker. "While you still can! Five! Four! Thr–"

Plastic rifles clattered to the ground. Hands shot up into the red glow of the fires. "We give up!" a man called. Submission became a wave sweeping over the panicked men.

"No," Teresa said. "Goddammit. No. We were so close. What kind of men are you...." She sat heavily. Hugged her knees. Her gaze fell to the blood-smeared grass as if she didn't see. She showed no sign of hearing the cries of the wounded or the crackle of the burning canoes.

Now, Stone told Caitlyn. *Before they rally.*

He emerged from cover, brandished his assault rifle. "If you can move, lie face down, arms and legs stretched out. Do it!"

Men went belly-down on the dirt. Stone spoke over his shoulder. "Check the wounded."

Shoulders square, Caitlyn strode to the man burned by her first throw. Stone approached the nearest clump of prisoners. He kicked away dropped rifles and glowered at the last few men still showing their faces. They gulped and joined the rest. As they moved, the flames engulfing the canoes lit up their faces, tinging mixed expressions of cowardice and guilt with red.

Only Teresa showed her face. Still seated, she looked at the ground. Flickering light showed her fingers interlaced in front of her shins.

Stone stepped toward her, checking for weapons on or near her. "You too."

She turned her head up. "You bastard," she said, voice empty. "I should have killed you in the trailer."

Nearby, men lifted their heads minimally from the dirt, angling their ears toward Teresa. An intuition told Stone how best to resolve the situation for the UN's sake. "I could say I know what it feels like to fail so badly." He smirked. "But I never have."

He walked past her, toward the prone men lying between her and the road. They burrowed their faces against the soil. Stone kicked plastic rifles toward the live oaks. Over the clatter of tumbling plastic, he kept his attention on any sounds that might come from behind him.

Something slowly whisked across a surface. A foot padded.

Stone kicked the next plastic rifle.

Another footfall, harder, faster.

He spun on his planted foot and raised the rifle.

A blur of hair. A glitter of flame reflected in a black alloy knife.

He fired a burst. All three rounds caught Teresa in the chest. The momentum of her run carried her forward and she had strength enough left to stab downward. Hate and rage yanked her lips back from snarling teeth.

Stone sidestepped and shoved her in the back. She stumbled to the ground, rolling onto her back. The knife slipped from weakening fingers. Blood flooded the soil from her torn chest.

A heart shot. She'd bleed to death in seconds.

He went to her. "The UN was always going to win," he said. "You're dying for nothing."

Her eyes looked glassy. She managed a minimal shake of her head. "I die free." She gagged. Blood like black oil oozed from her mouth. "Not a slave."

One last spasm of her lithe body. One last gasp choking on blood. Then her body lay still. Reflections of flames from the burning canoes danced in Teresa's vacant eyes.

The Jezhek persona shoved its thoughts into Stone's mind. *You're a goddam murderer.*

Stone straightened up and his mind pulled clear of the Jezhek persona. Twinges racked his limbs and body. He'd be sore tomorrow. Not for the first time. Wouldn't be the last.

Smoke thickened the air over the canoes and drifted closer, mixing with the stench of spilled blood and burnt flesh. The prisoners remained with bellies down and faces buried against the dirt. The surrendered men hunched their shoulders and pulled their heads down like frightened turtles.

With Teresa dead, they would go meekly to jail. All the people of Freeland would bow under the UN's yoke. Despite his fatigue and adrenaline hangover, a wolfish smile slipped onto his face.

"I've called in local police and ambulance services," Caitlyn said, "along with local UN officials." She stopped near Stone and nodded at Teresa's corpse. *I see you got what you wanted.*

She wanted to speak frankly without prisoners overhearing. *She was the last chance for a viable resistance against us. Her death is for the best.*

A second later, Caitlyn laughed aloud. She slapped her knee. Nearby prisoners flinched.

What the hell? Stone asked.

Through her visor, her hazel eyes regarded him from under raised eyebrows. *You enticed her to attack you for the good of the UN. Nothing personal at all.*

Stone glowered at her. *You think I enjoyed killing her?*

"No," she said, quietly but with a firm edge. "I know you did."

EPILOGUE

Outside Gray's office, the bellies of gray clouds brushed the roofs of skyscrapers over the Upper East Side and muffled a sun low in the sky over Brooklyn. An ugly winter day in Manhattan, but after the vast unpeopled landscapes of Freeland, the low clouds and angular lines of the city comforted Stone like a blanket as he eased into one of the chairs facing his boss' desk.

Gray raised a coffee mug and turned his impassive gaze across the broad cherry surface. "An adequate operation, Stone."

"You're getting generous with your praise." Stone raised a glass of sparkling water to his mouth. The overused muscles of his arm ached as he sipped. A lemon wedge touched his lip and wafted tart citrus scent to his nose. The whiff of lemon perked him up slightly, yet the wormhole equivalent of jet lag and last night's red-eye from Houston still sanded his eyes.

"Before you left for Freeland, you gave yourself three assignments. You completed two of them."

Stone frowned. Too early in the morning, too many aches distracting him. "Remind me."

"For one, you determined Dragon's cause of death."

A yawn, then Stone nodded. Prisoner interrogations led to the arrest of Thomas Benavides and the uncovering of a shallow grave in the Benavides' bioseeding concession far to the southeast of Svoboda City. The corpse's SNP profile matched Dragon. Unless Teresa's team had a CRISPR dermal vector and knew how to use it...

Stone rubbed his eyes with his free hand and sipped sparkling water.

"And for another," Gray said, "you discovered and neutralized the Benavides family's missile launcher. The preliminary report from the forensic techs indicates she had a decent chance of destroying the wormhole."

The earlier conversation in this same room—seemingly months earlier, but no more than four or five days—trickled back into Stone's mind. "I couldn't find the UN turncoat."

Gray set down his mug. His fingers lingered on the handle, until he fixed his cold eyes on Stone. "You did prove a UN employee on Freeland provided intelligence and know-how to Teresa Benavides. We'll sift the databases regarding every UN employee stationed on-planet for further clues. We'll find him."

"Good."

Gray peered down his nose at the old-fashioned LED display embedded in his desk. "I see you opted to work with an ITB agent. What's your assessment of Ms. Fredriksen?"

Stone's eyebrows knitted. Fredriksen? Caitlyn. "She was adequate, especially at analysis and data gathering. She'd been trained at wet work but needs more practice."

"If you had the option, would you work with her again?"

"We're collaborating with the keyhole kops now?"

Gray lifted the fingers of his right hand off the desk and waved them like a card player declining another card. "Preferably not. Yet I must be prepared in case working with ITB should ever prove the least bad option."

After a sip of sparkling water, Stone said, "Sure."

"You sound unconvinced."

Stone shrugged. "She can be a little mouthy at times. But if she ever overdid, I could smack it out of her."

One of Gray's eyebrows arched upward. "Small wonder women

find you irresistible." He reached for his coffee mug. "I have nothing more. Follow the standard post-operation protocol, then take the rest of the week off."

"Thanks." Stone drained the rest of his sparkling water, then slid his rump forward on his chair with stiff motions of his legs. "One thing before I go."

Gray lowered his mug below his chin. "Certainly."

"A new tech–Fabio? No, Fabrizio–prepared my cover story. The persona was too intrusive. I want my old tech, Jürgen, back in charge of the cover stories for my next operations."

"I'll take that under advisement." Gray remained expressionless. "Anything further?"

He mused for a moment, but wormhole lag and multiple nights of little sleep short-circuited his thoughts. "No."

"Enjoy your time off. Good luck coaching those boys at football."

Stone blinked. "I didn't know you cared."

"About football? No." Gray's long face moved in a minimal nod. "But even when I have no assignment for you, the future of the UN lies in your hands."

Just a few days earlier, but it seemed like months. Vikram, Hamza, Edwin, and the others, shivering in the snow. Stone chuckled, and his world felt a little more normal. "They're good boys, but better the UN's future lies in my hands than their hips."

ABOUT THE AUTHOR

I'm **Raymund Eich.** I use my Middle American upbringing as a launchpad for journeys to the ends of the Universe.

Growing up in the Midwest prepared me for my academic career, culminating with a Ph.D. in biochemistry from Rice University. It helps me help inventors prosper from their progress in medicine, biotechnology, and green energy.

Above all, it inspires me to write science fiction and fantasy about ordinary people facing extraordinary wonders and horrors, battling enemies both foreign and domestic, and building better lives for themselves, their families, and their societies.

My last name has one syllable and is pronounced "eye-sh." I live in Houston with my family.

Connect with me at **www.raymundeich.com** or follow the QR code below.

Online and brick-and-mortar bookstores around the world list millions of books, with thousands more published every day. I'm glad you discovered this one.

If you'd like to know when I release a new book, instead of leaving it to chance, join my Readers Club. I'll email you from time to time with publishing news, off-beat patents, a short personal update, or a reminder about an older book of mine you might have missed.

Yes, please! I'll go to **www.raymundeich.com/mailing-list** or scan the QR code below.

No thanks. I'll take my chances next time I look for your books.

OTHER BOOKS BY THE AUTHOR

Available wherever books are sold.

Learn more about these titles at our website, **www.cv2books.com,** or follow the QR code below.

STONE CHALMERS

Earth barely survived the 21st Century.

Biotechnological and nuclear terrorism, civil war, famine, and ethnic cleansing killed billions. Thousands fled on warpdrive ships to colonize planets around distant suns.

In the 22nd century, after Earth unified under one world government, it opened wormhole links to the distant colonies, to prevent a repeat of the previous century's chaos on a galactic scale.

Enter operative Stone Chalmers. Spy. Assassin. Instrument maintaining Earth's dominion over all human worlds.

Opposing him are hostile forces on colony worlds… and within the Earth government itself.

When Stone clashes with those forces, Earth—and every human world—will be transformed forever.

Learn more about the Stone Chalmers series at **www.cv2books.com/stone-chalmers**, or follow the QR code below.

The Freeland Vendetta

On the newly rediscovered colony world Freeland, a conspiracy plans a powerful blow against Earth's control of the planet. A blow supported by treacherous forces inside the government of Earth.

The Trinity Deception

From the religious colony world of Trinity come clues of a long-lost prize. The last warpdrive ship outside Earth's control.

The Minerva Conspiracy

Expecting a mission beneath his talents, Stone fights for his life—and soul—against a terrifying conspiracy.

The Terra Betrayal

Schemes and plots from the colonies and the capital converge in the halls of power on Earth itself. Only Stone can fight his way through a web of intrigue and bring freedom to all human worlds.

THE INCEPTI CATACLYSM

The entire galaxy knows about the Incepti Cataclysm. The occupation force from Vela destroyed a planet with nanotechnology. Only a few Inceptis fled the wave of death in time to join their brethren scattered across the Democracy.

Everything the galaxy knows is a lie.

Anara Orden. Daughter of survivors. Recruited by fellow Inceptis to join Democracy intelligence. Though young and good of heart, she kills without qualms. She knows her employers only order her to terminate Velan agents threatening the Democracy.

But when her next target is a fellow Incepti, she questions everything and chooses a new mission. She will share the truth with friend and foe alike.

Yet powerful forces across the galaxy will do whatever it takes to cling to power. Even if millions of innocents must die.

Escape from Conatus (Book One)

When Anara learns the truth, a simple mission becomes a flight for survival.

Revelation in Vela (Book Two)

Instead of a refuge, Anara and her companions end up in the cross-hairs—of two sides.

Victory for Carina (Book Three)

As war comes to the galaxy, only Anara's desperate plan can bring a just and lasting peace.

THE FALSE FLAG WAR

Concordia's mission reflected the best of the human race. Crew and scientists from both of Earth's rival factions, Humanists and Traditionalists, journeyed for years at relativistic speeds to reach Bravo Charlie, a life-bearing planet orbiting Alpha Centauri B, to expand the frontiers of knowledge for all.

Concordia's mission also reflected humanity at its worst. Corrupt bureaucrats and ambitious political leaders in both factions maintained a status quo backed by weapons of mass destruction. The faction commanders on the mission each sought to seize advantages for their side alone.

Then the ship received transmissions. Signs of an ancient, powerful alien presence on the planet below.

Exploration 2127

Sent to explore, **Jaeger** and **McIlroy**, born and raised in a Texas divided by razor wire and minefields. Men torn between the mission's ideals and orders from their respective faction commanders, oily Varanathan and domineering Sandford.

Then Jaeger and McIlroy discover how to bring Earth's factions together... using knowledge given by aliens dead over a million years.

Invasion 2132

Concordia fell silent. Mission control now detects an unknown ship leaving the Alpha Centauri system. Heading to Earth at relativistic speeds. Silent about its purpose. Its crew unknown.

Earth's one chance: Its rival factions must work for mutual defense, against shadowy figures who strive to use the unknown ship for their own faction's gain.

THE CONFEDERATED WORLDS

The purpose of all other combat arms is to put the infantryman in sole possession of the battlefield.

A thousand years from now, while Earth sleeps in virtual reality, three polities—the Confederated Worlds, the Unity, and the Progressive Republic—strive to connect the scattered, terraformed worlds of humankind by artificial wormholes.

When they meet, they clash, in a decades-long struggle of arms that will embroil every human world, in which dedication to duty liberates worlds—and oneself.

Learn more about the Confederated Worlds series at **www.cv2books.com/the-confederated-worlds**, or follow the QR code below.

Take the Shilling

The Confederated Worlds implanted in his brain the skills to make him a soldier. Tomas Neumann had to learn for himself how to survive interstellar war.

Operation Iago

The Confederated Worlds lost the war. Can Lt. Tomas Neumann win the peace against elusive, deceptive foes out to turn the Confederated Worlds against itself?

A Bodyguard of Lies

Assigned to the halls of power, only Capt. Tomas Neumann can save the Confederated Worlds from the ultimate treachery.

OTHER NOVELS

The Blank Slate

Neuroscience entrepreneur Clay Shieffer must stop a tyrannical president…
because he unwittingly gave the tyrant power over the human mind.

New California

After New California's founder committed suicide, two men vied to rule the
colony.

Ashwin George, supported by the colony's elite and the Chinese company
dominating half the settled galaxy.

Against him, Desmond Park, nanotechnology engineer, armed with the most
formidable weapon of all.

A single idea.

The Reincarnation Run

Skeptical spacejock Landry Krieger knows exactly how to smuggle the
"reborn" spiritual leader of an oppressed people past their conquerors... but
the boy's priests—and governess—shake up his orderly plans.

Azureseas: Cantrell's War

Ross Cantrell joined the animal control mission on the newly-discovered
planet Azureseas to earn the money to start married life together with his
girlfriend.

Then Ross discovers the truth about the planet's "animals."

SHORT NOVELS

Love and Death in the City of Bone

He had a month to learn the planet's mysteries—and Juliette's.

His cover story: return to Elard to dismantle his sect's missionary work to the planet's natives.

His true mission: investigate decades-old mysteries of love and death.

His objective: return to Earth with his discovery.

If he can.

A Mighty Fortress

Theodore and his team from the Lutheran Interstellar Terraforming Society would transform a barren, rocky world into a refuge of faith and life.

Or die trying.

Winner and the Poacher

A Portia Oakeshott, Dinosaur Veterinarian Short Novel

As a consultant to law enforcement, Portia confronts stark evidence of a rich young man's crime: the mounted head of a massive herbivorous *Wintonotitan*. A winner.

A dinosaur the company never granted a permit for hunting.

SHORT STORY COLLECTIONS

The First Voyages: The Complete Science Fiction Stories 1998-2012

From 21st century asteroid settlements to World War II Romania, from an Earth dominated by immortal aliens to Christ's empty tomb, a fresh, distinctive voice in science fiction will take you on journeys to the photosphere of the sun, the coding regions of DNA, and the complexities of the human psyche.

Stage Separations: The Complete Science Fiction Stories 2013-2018

In these pages, you can...

...race against time to solve mysteries hidden in a planet's vast desert—and in a woman's heart

...learn the true story of a president's assassination

...journey 14,000 miles to a high-tech fountain of youth

...win or go "home"—to an Earth you've never seen

and explore six other worlds created by a distinctive voice in twenty-first century science fiction.

Orbital Maneuvers: The Complete Science Fiction Stories 2019-2020

In these pages, you can join–

A mission to terraform a lifeless, rocky planet | A private detective uncovering the ultimate crime | A woman called by an ex-boyfriend… who's been dead twenty years | A President breaking his country's highest law | A star athlete discovering the true price of a championship

–and enjoy five more tales, in the latest installment of the Complete Science Fiction Stories of Raymund Eich.

Extravehicular Activities: The Complete Science Fiction Stories 2021-2022

Leave the safety of your space capsule for the dangers of billion-year old alien derelicts, intelligent insects with mysterious motives, espionage in an alternate 1920s Paris, and rogue reconstructed dinosaurs.

These wonders and more await in the fourth volume of the Complete Science Fiction Stories of Raymund Eich.